"I wish all Holmesian pastiche could be as honest, as knowledgeable, as enthusiastic and as well written – in short, as good – as these children's books."

THE SHERLOCK HOLMES SOCIETY OF LONDON

Other Baker Street Boys adventures:

THE CASE OF THE HAUNTED HORRORS

ANTHONY READ

illustrated by

DAVID FRANKLAND

WALKER
BOOKS

For Elliot and Oliver, Jack and Miranda

First published 2009 by Walker Books Ltd
87 Vauxhall Walk, London SE11 5HJ

This edition published 2012

2 4 6 8 10 9 7 5 3 1

Text © 2009 Anthony Read
Illustrations © 2009 David Frankland

The right of Anthony Read and David Frankland to be identified as author
and illustrator respectively of this work has been asserted by them in
accordance with the Copyright, Designs and Patents Act 1988

This book has been typeset in ITC Garamond

Printed and bound in Italy by 🦁 Grafica Veneta S.p.A.

British Library Cataloguing in Publication Data:
a catalogue record for this book is available from the British Library

ISBN 978-1-4063-3635-1

www.walker.co.uk

Contents

A *jagged flash of lightning tore open the*
night sky over Baker Street. For a moment
it was as though someone had switched on a
giant floodlight, lighting up the buildings below
– then, just as suddenly, it was gone and every-
thing was even darker than before. The lightning
was followed almost immediately by a crash of
thunder that sounded like a thousand cannons
being fired at once.

"Blimey, that was a close 'un!" exclaimed
Sarge. The old soldier usually counted the sec-
onds between flash and thunder, to tell how far
away the lightning was – five seconds for every
mile, he reckoned. This time there had been no
gap, which meant it must be right overhead.
He looked anxiously around, to see if anything
had been struck. Then, hanging on tightly with

his one good hand to the pitcher of beer he was carrying home from the pub, he hurried back to the Baker Street Bazaar.

As he pushed through the wrought-iron gates and hurried into his lodge, the deep rumble of the thunder echoed overhead like a roll of drums. Strangely, though, there was no sign of rain. Another lightning flash and a bang as loud as a volley from all the guns of the Royal Artillery made him jump so hard that some of the beer slopped over the edge of the jug and splashed onto the floor.

"My oath!" he cried. "It's enough to waken the dead."

Sarge put the pitcher carefully down on the table and reached for a cloth to wipe up the spilt beer. As he straightened, he glanced out of the door and along the Bazaar to Madame Dupont's waxworks exhibition – and froze. There was a dim light moving behind one of the windows.

"Hello," he said to himself. "What's goin' on? Looks like somebody's in there!"

Tucking a truncheon under the stump of his amputated left arm, he lifted a bunch of keys from their hook on the wall, picked up his bull's-eye lantern and set off to investigate.

The waxworks gallery was always a bit spooky at night. Standing in their shadowy alcoves around the wall, the wax figures often looked as though they might be coming to life. But Sarge was used to this, and it did not worry him. He shone his lantern around the room in case an intruder was hiding among the models. There was no one. Then he heard a sound – the quiet, stealthy sound of someone moving. It came not from the main exhibition, but from the side room that Madame Dupont had recently turned into the Dungeon of Horrors.

Sarge was not a nervous man, nor was he very imaginative. But he didn't like going into the Dungeon, particularly at night and on his own. True to its name, this gallery was full of horrors: lifelike – or perhaps death-like – wax figures of murderers and their victims splashed with gore; unspeakable monsters and deformed creatures so revolting they made your stomach turn. It was so scary that Madame Dupont had offered a prize of the princely sum of five pounds to anyone who would spend a whole night alone in there. So far, no one had dared to take up the challenge. Could it be, Sarge wondered, that somebody was doing so now? Or was there a more sinister explanation?

Seeing light seeping through the crack under the heavy oak door to the Dungeon, Sarge summoned up his courage, took a deep breath and gave the door a cautious push. It creaked loudly as it opened – a sound effect that Madame Dupont had installed especially to make people nervous. Inside the room, someone or something moved. The beam from Sarge's bull's-eye lantern swept over the wax models, picking out a headless corpse, a grinning skull and finally the agonized face of the murder victim in Madame Dupont's latest tableau. Next to it stood the figure of another man, his face lit eerily from below. And it was the same face.

Sarge let out a yell and screwed his eyes tight shut. When he opened them again, there was no one there. Only a thin wisp of smoke hung in the air. The figure had disappeared.

SEEING A GHOST

The morning dawned bright and sunny, with no sign of the previous night's electric storm. The Baker Street Boys were cheerful as they left HQ, their secret cellar home, for another day on the streets of London. Rosie, the little flower girl, filled her tray with posies for the ladies and buttonholes for the gentlemen, and set off to sell them on bustling Baker Street. Shiner headed for Paddington railway station carrying a green wooden box holding his boot polishes, brushes and cloths. Queenie started on her round of shops – grocers, greengrocers, butchers, bakers – looking for yesterday's leftovers to beg or buy cheaply from friendly shopkeepers to turn into one of her tasty stews. Everything seemed like a very normal, ordinary morning – until Wiggins,

Beaver, Gertie and Sparrow strolled up to the Baker Street Bazaar.

As they approached the entrance gates, they were surprised to see a small crowd of people on the pavement outside. Most of them were the owners of the little shops that lined the inside of the Bazaar, plus a couple of coachmen whose carriages were parked inside. At the front was the unmistakable figure of Madame Dupont, wearing a vivid purple cloak over an equally bright red satin dress. The tall green ostrich feathers in her hat swayed backwards and forwards as she pushed and tugged at the heavy iron gates and shouted for Sarge to open them.

Being an old soldier, Sarge was usually up and about long before anybody else. It was unheard of for him not to be "on parade", as he always put it, bright and early. But on this morning there was no sign of him, and the big gates were still firmly locked.

As the four Boys arrived from one direction, PC Higgins appeared from the other.

"'Ello, 'ello!" the burly policeman called out. "What's goin' on here, then?"

"Ah, officer," Madame Dupont greeted him. "We are locked out. Locked out of our own businesses. It's a disgrace!"

"That's not like Sergeant Scroggs," said PC Higgins, pushing back his helmet.

"D'you think something's happened to him?" Wiggins asked.

"Could have."

"But there's no way we can find out without getting in," said Madame Dupont impatiently. "And the keys are in his lodge."

"That's soon fixed," said Wiggins. "Gertie here could be over that gate in two shakes of a dog's tail. Climb anything, she can."

"Is that right?" PC Higgins looked suspiciously at the tousle-haired girl in boys' clothes.

"Sure and haven't I been cloimbin' trees since I was knee-high to a grasshopper?" Gertie told him with a cheeky Irish grin. "Shall I show you?"

"Go on, then," grunted the policeman.

"And just get a move on," Madame Dupont snapped. "We're sick of having to wait here like ninnies."

Wiggins and Beaver gave Gertie a leg-up, and

in no time at all she had hopped over the gate and down the other side, run to the lodge and knocked on the door. When there was no answer, she lifted the latch and opened it.

"The keys should be hanging up just inside," Wiggins called to her. "The one for the gates is the biggest."

Gertie stepped in and reached for the key, then let out a shriek.

"What is it?" Wiggins asked as she came tumbling out of the door, clutching the key and looking pale. "What's up?"

"It's ... it's Sarge..." she cried. "I think ... I think he's dead!"

There was a gasp from the little crowd. Gertie's hands were shaking so much that she couldn't get the big key into the keyhole, so Wiggins reached through the bars and took it from her.

"What's he look like?" he asked as he unlocked the gate from the outside.

"He's stretched out on the floor, all stiff and still."

"Everybody stay where you are," PC Higgins ordered. "This is a job for the police." He pushed through the gates and went into the lodge, placing his large boots very carefully so as not to disturb any possible evidence. The others watched breathlessly and waited for him to emerge, which he did very shortly.

"Well?" demanded Madame Dupont. "Is he dead?"

"Dead *drunk*," PC Higgins replied, holding up an empty bottle. "What you might describe, ma'am, as paralytic."

"Drunk on duty!" Madame Dupont declared, trembling with indignation. "It's a disgrace! The man's clearly not to be trusted. I shall see to it that he is dismissed from his post and never works again."

"That's for you to decide, ma'am. It's not a police matter."

"Poor old Sarge," said Beaver. "Ain't there nothin' we can do for him?"

"Only one thing you can do, lad," the policeman replied. "Make him as comfortable as you can and let him sleep it off. Now, if you'll excuse me, folks, I shall return to *my* duties." And after touching his helmet in a salute to Madame

Dupont and the others, he turned away and plodded off down the street.

From round the corner came the sound of one of the little German bands that could regularly be seen and heard on London's streets, and soon afterwards the four musicians appeared, wearing military-style uniforms and playing a jolly oom-pah tune as they marched slowly along the pavement. Their leader paused to give the policeman a smart salute and held out his collecting box as he passed them, but PC Higgins kept his hands firmly behind his back.

The Boys just about managed to lift Sarge from the floor and onto his bed. He mumbled something in his sleep about a dead man walking, but he didn't wake up and they decided to do what the policeman had suggested and leave him where he was.

"Can't understand it," said Wiggins. "I know Sarge likes a glass of beer or two, but I ain't never seen him blotto. Not even a bit tipsy."

"P'raps somethin' upset him," said Sparrow.

"You mean he was like drownin' his sorrows, ain't that what people say?" asked Beaver.

"My da used to do that sometimes," said Gertie, "when he was thinkin' about my poor ma and how much he missed her."

"P'raps Sarge was missin' his arm," said Sparrow. "Or his days in the army, with all his mates."

Later in the day, when they went back, the four Boys found Sarge awake and nursing a bad headache – and they discovered that the reason he had drunk a whole bottle of spirits was something quite different from what they had thought.

"I seen a ghost," he told them. "In the Dungeon of Horrors. It was that chap what murdered his wife and done hisself in. Madame's latest tableau."

The Boys stared at him, open-mouthed.

"You mean the waxwork come to life?" Beaver asked.

"No! It weren't the waxwork – it were *him*," Sarge groaned, holding his throbbing head. "Standin' right next to it. Large as life and no mistake."

"But he's dead … ain't he?" asked Sparrow.

"And buried," Sarge asserted. "And if he hadn't done hisself in, they'd have hanged him for murder anyhow."

"So you reckon you seen his ghost?" said

Wiggins, thinking hard. "What exac'ly was he doing when you spied him?"

"Doin'? He weren't doing nothin'. Just stood there, starin' at me, like *he* was the one what'd seen a ghost."

"I see. Then what?"

"Then he vanished. Like in a puff of smoke."

"Cor," Sparrow breathed. "No wonder you wanted a drink."

"Trouble is, when I'd had one drink I wanted another. And my jug was empty."

"You didn't get like that on one jug of beer, though," said Wiggins.

"No – I always keeps a bottle of brandy in the cupboard, in case of emergencies. Like if a lady or gent was to come over all faint."

"And this was an emergency?"

"Well, it ain't every day a chap sees a real live ghost, is it?"

"Or even a dead one," Sparrow joked, then quickly shut up as the others glared at him.

"Well, live or dead, he's done for me," Sarge moaned. "Madame Dupont says as soon as Lord Holdhurst comes back next week she'll get him to sack me. I'll have no job and no home."

"She can't do that!" Beaver protested.

"She says I must've been seein' things 'cos I was drunk. But I weren't drunk when I seen that ghost. Only afterwards. I swear!"

"We believe you, Sarge," Wiggins told him.

"Yeah, but will His Lordship?"

"We'll tell him," said Sparrow. "He knows us from when we saved Ravi and the Ranjipur Ruby."

"It's no good. He won't listen to you."

"Then we'll find somebody he *will* listen to," said Wiggins. "Don't you fret – just leave it to the Baker Street Boys."

Billy opened the door of 221b Baker Street and looked down his snub nose at the four Boys standing on the step.

"Oh, it's you," he sneered. "What d'you want?"

"Hello, Billy. That's a fine way to welcome your old mates what saved your bacon after them Chinamen pinched Mrs Hudson's valuable ornament," Wiggins said cheerfully. "I see it's back in its rightful place," he added, pointing at the jade dragon standing on the hall table.

The pageboy turned to look at it, and nodded.

"Yeah, well, thanks," he said grudgingly. "Mrs H was pleased about that. Now, what can I do for you? Mr Holmes ain't here. He's away on a case."

"Like he always is," chuckled Wiggins. "But it ain't him we're after. We want to see Dr Watson."

"Then you're in luck. 'Cos he's just got back from his rounds. I'll see if he's at home."

"What you talkin' about?" said Gertie. "You just said he was."

"What I said was, he's in the house. Being 'at home' means he's prepared to receive visitors. That's how it's done in polite society," Billy sniffed.

"Never mind all that," said Wiggins. "Just go and tell him we're here and we gotta talk to him about something, and it can't wait."

Billy trotted off upstairs and returned a moment later to usher them up to the rooms Dr Watson shared with Sherlock Holmes.

"Now, then, my young friends," the doctor greeted them. "What is it you want to see me about that's so urgent?"

"It's Sarge," Wiggins blurted out.

"Sarge?" The doctor looked puzzled. "Oh, you

mean Sergeant Scroggs?"

"He's in trouble. Big trouble. And we thought, seeing as you told us how he saved your life on the Khyber, you'd want to help him."

"Indeed I would, if it's within my power. Tell me what this trouble is."

"They're gonna sack him and throw him out of his home," Sparrow blurted out.

"All because he seen a ghost," added Gertie.

"But if he hadn't seen the ghost, he wouldn't have needed a drink," Beaver joined in, his words tumbling out helter-skelter, "and if his beer hadn't all gone he wouldn't have needed the brandy what he kept in case of emergencies, and if he hadn't—"

"Wait, wait!" cried Dr Watson, holding up his hands to silence them. "You're making my head spin. One at a time, if you please."

"Right," Wiggins said, taking command. "You three be quiet and leave this to me. It's like this, Doctor. When we went round the Bazaar this morning, we see Madame Dupont and all the shop-keepers and coachmen standing outside the gates, what was locked 'cos Sarge was still asleep. Only he wasn't just asleep, he was spark out. Sozzled."

"Ah, he was inebriated."

"Eh?"

"Drunk."

"That's right. Like you say, Doctor. Inebrified."

"A very serious offence for a soldier, being drunk on duty."

"Yeah, we know that. But he had good reason."

"He'd seen a ghost, you say?"

"That's right. In the Dungeon of Horrors last night. The ghost of the bloke what murdered his wife then topped hisself."

The doctor nodded. "I can understand a man needing to fortify himself after an experience like that. He might well find such an apparition somewhat unnerving."

"Exac'ly. Only Madame Dupont don't see it like that. She reckons he must have been drunk already and that's why he was imagining things."

"And we know he wasn't," Gertie burst in, unable to contain herself any longer. "He's not like that, is Sarge. He never gets drunk and he never tells lies."

Dr Watson stroked his chin thoughtfully. "I quite

agree – it's not like the Sergeant Scroggs I know."

"If he had been drunk, he'd have owned up and took his medicine," Sparrow declared. "It's not right. We gotta help him."

"Very well," said Dr Watson. "I shall see what I can do. Perhaps I could have a word with Lord Holdhurst. I believe his family owns the Bazaar."

"We tried that already," said Wiggins. "We went round his house, but they said he was on his estate in Scotland till next week."

"So we got till then to sort it out," Gertie said, brightening up.

"We better had," said Beaver. "'Cos if we don't, when Lord H gets back he'll give poor old Sarge the boot."

Dr Watson agreed to go and see Sarge and also to talk to Madame Dupont and the shopkeepers. When he spoke to his old comrade, however, Sarge was adamant that he really had seen a ghost and that he had not got drunk until afterwards. Dr Watson gave him a thorough examination but could find nothing wrong, apart from a bad hangover. Knowing Sarge to be honest and trustworthy, the doctor believed him. But although he did his best to persuade Madame Dupont and the others, they refused to budge. The businessmen (and women) of the Bazaar were determined to report Sarge to Lord Holdhurst and demand that he be sacked. They could not trust a drunken man to guard their premises, they said – especially one who claimed to see ghosts.

Gathered in HQ that evening, the Boys were depressed and downhearted. Not even the fact that Queenie had managed to find some tasty scrag-end of mutton to go into her stew could raise their spirits. The idea that their friend was about to lose both his job and his home was too much to bear.

"If only there was *somethin'* we could do to help him," wailed Rosie.

The others nodded glumly, then after a moment's silence Wiggins suddenly perked up. "Hang on," he said. "P'raps there is!"

"What?" asked Beaver.

"Well," Wiggins began, "they all say Sarge *imagined* seeing that ghost 'cos he was drunk, right?"

"Right," said Queenie. "'Cos they don't believe there is a ghost."

"But what if somebody else – somebody what was stone-cold sober – was to go in there at night and see it?"

The other Boys stared at Wiggins in admiration. Then doubt crept in as light dawned.

"You don't mean...?" Rosie began.

"Us?" Shiner concluded. "Oh, no. Ain't no way I'm gonna spend the night in that dungeon with no spook."

"You don't have to," said Wiggins. "It wouldn't do for all of us to go. That might scare the ghost off."

"Yeah, I dare say it would," said Gertie, sounding relieved.

"But there'd have to be more than one, or nobody'd believe us. So that's me and somebody else..."

There was a pause, then Beaver bravely volunteered. "Me," he said. "I'll come with you."

"Good lad. Come on, let's get round there now."

IN THE DUNGEON

"You wouldn't catch me spendin' the night in there, not for all the tea in China," Sarge told Wiggins and Beaver as he unlocked the door to Madame Dupont's waxwork museum. "You're very brave lads, and I appreciate what you're doin'."

"We couldn't just let 'em kick you out and do nothin', could we," said Beaver.

"There's a good many as would," replied Sarge. "Maybe I should come in with you…"

"No, you shouldn't," Wiggins said firmly. "If we're gonna prove there really *is* a ghost in there, and not just in your imagination, we gotta be able to say we seen it for ourselves, without you. Right?"

"I suppose so. But you take care. I'd never

forgive myself if anythin' happened to you."

"Don't worry," Wiggins told him. "It's only an old ghost, ain't it? Anyway, there's two of us. We'll look out for each other. Right, Beav?"

"Right," said Beaver, trying to sound confident, but the word came out as a squeak. He cleared his throat noisily.

"Come on, then," said Wiggins, pretending not to notice. He checked his trusty bull's-eye lantern and stepped through the door. Beaver followed, sticking close to him.

Inside, Madame Dupont's Red Indian brave stood guard, threatening them with his tomahawk. The Boys were not afraid; they had seen him too many times before. But the main hall was dim and full of shadows, and the flickering of the gas jets, which had been turned down low for the night, caused some of the waxwork figures to look as though they might be moving. This made both Boys nervous, but they pressed on boldly towards the heavy barred doors of the Dungeon, wondering what horrors it would hold.

"That door could do with a spot of oil," observed Beaver as it creaked open.

"It's s'posed to sound like that," Wiggins replied.

"It made me jump."

"That's the idea."

"Oh, yeah. See what you mean."

The gas lamps here had been turned down so low that it was very dark indeed, with big patches of shadow in which nothing could be seen and anything could be lurking. The Boys had never been inside the Dungeon before, and they looked around open-mouthed as the beam of Wiggins's lantern picked out macabre scenes from the blackness.

They gasped at the gruesome sight of an old, rotten gibbet, from which dangled the skeletal body of a dead highwayman in a metal cage, its flesh long decayed away, its bones covered with the tattered remnants of clothing, its blackened teeth bared in a ghastly grimace beneath the empty eye sockets. They trembled at an ancient Egyptian mummy, swathed in bandages, which looked as though it were about to sit up in its painted sarcophagus. They shuddered at the sight of a Tudor executioner, his face half hidden by a black mask, holding aloft the head of a queen, which he had just severed from her body with his bloodied axe.

Further back, the light from the lantern glistened on the blade of a guillotine from the French Revolution, about to fall on the neck of a hapless aristocrat. And in another corner a medieval torturer lowered a red-hot poker towards a half-naked man stretched on a rack, his face twisted in a soundless scream.

Some of the scenes were from more recent times. The infamous Jack the Ripper, shown slashing a young woman with a long knife, had committed several murders in the East End barely ten years earlier and was still feared in the area. But the newest tableau was of a crime that had taken place only a few months ago, and which was still fresh in people's minds. It showed a man in his mid-thirties about to shoot himself with a revolver after murdering his wife and child – and it was *his* ghost that Sarge had seen the night before.

The scene was very realistic – Madame Dupont had bought up all the things that had been in the man's study, where the murders had been committed, and she had recreated every detail with the help of photographs taken by the police at the time. Prints of the photos were displayed alongside the tableau, to show everyone how clever she had been. Wiggins and Beaver stared at them, and felt a fluttering in their stomachs at the thought that while all the characters in the scene were just wax models, these black-and-white pictures were of actual dead people.

"Urgh! Gruesome," said Beaver. He turned back to the figure of the man with the revolver. "D'you think that's really what happened?"

"I dare say," Wiggins answered.

"But what if it wasn't? What if that's why the geezer come back?"

"How d'you mean?"

"P'raps he wanted to tell people what *really* happened. I mean, if everybody says he done it, when really he didn't, he wouldn't be able to rest easy, would he?"

"You mean he'd want to come back from beyond the grave to set things straight, like?"

"Exac'ly. Wouldn't you?"

Wiggins thought about this for a moment, then grinned. "Well," he said, "if he comes back again tonight you can ask him."

Beaver wasn't too sure that he'd want to speak to a ghost – or even that he'd dare to. So he said nothing, and the two Boys crouched down in a corner, out of sight behind the guillotine and the doomed French aristocrat. Wiggins closed the cover of his lantern and they waited, nervously, in the darkness. It was deathly quiet. Even the tiny squeak of a mouse and the skittering of its feet on the floorboards seemed to echo around the Dungeon like the noise of stampeding cattle. And when the clock in the main gallery struck the hour, it sounded to the Boys like Big Ben itself. Wiggins counted the chimes under his breath – ten, eleven ... twelve.

"Midnight," he whispered to Beaver. "Watch out now. This is when ghosts walk."

Right on cue, they heard a faint noise outside. The sound of a muffled footstep. Wiggins held his breath. Beaver clenched his teeth to stop them chattering. Then came an eerie creak.

"That's funny," murmured Wiggins. "I didn't

think ghosts needed to open doors. I thought they walked right through 'em."

He raised his head very carefully and watched as a dark shape materialized in the doorway. It moved across the Dungeon and stopped by the new tableau. There was the scrape and flare of a match being struck, and then a softer light as a lantern was lit. The Boys could now see that it was held by a tall man, who began inspecting objects in the make-believe room, starting with a leather-bound book that lay on the desk. When he half turned, Wiggins saw that his face was indeed that of the murderer in the tableau, but ghostly pale. Unable to help himself, Wiggins let out a gasp.

The man spun round, raising his lantern higher. "Who's there?" he called sharply.

The two Boys stayed still as statues – or wax-works. They stopped breathing. They didn't even blink. But it was too late. The man knew they were there.

"Come out and show yourself, whoever you are!" he barked. "I warn you – I am armed."

Reluctantly, cautiously, the two Boys stood up. The man stared at them. They stared back at him.

He was tall, well-built and dark-haired, and wearing a long black coat.

"Children!" he exclaimed. "What on earth are you doing here?"

"'Ere, who you calling children?" Wiggins said boldly. "And come to that, what on earth are *you* doing here?"

"You ain't no ghost!" Beaver exclaimed.

"Why should I be a ghost?"

"'Cos … 'cos…" Beaver pointed a trembling finger at the waxwork figure.

The man looked at it, puzzled. Then his face cleared. "Ah," he said. "You thought I was…?"

"And we weren't the only ones," said Wiggins. "Our friend Sarge did as well. It *was* you he seen last night, wasn't it?"

"Sarge? Oh, you mean the commissionaire. Yes, I'm afraid it was. I'm sorry if I gave him a fright."

"You did more'n that," Wiggins said. "You cost him his job."

"In that case, I am truly, truly sorry."

Beaver stared at the man with deep hostility. "So you should be," he said. "And where's your gun?"

"I beg your pardon?"

"You said you was armed."

"So I did. I was lying."

"Why? Don't you know it's wrong to tell lies?" The man shrugged.

Wiggins smiled. "You was scared, wasn't you?"

"I confess I was. And that's the truth."

"What of? It ain't ghosts, is it?"

"No." He gave Wiggins a sharp look. "You're a very astute young chap. And very bold, too. Who are you?"

"My name is Wiggins. Arnold Wiggins. Captain of the Baker Street Boys. And Beaver here is my lieutenant."

"And what do they do, your Baker Street Boys?"

"We're special assistants to Mr Sherlock Holmes, the famous consulting detective."

"Sherlock Holmes! The very man I need."

"Well, he ain't around right now. So you'll have to make do with us."

"You?" The man gave a hollow laugh. "What could you do? A bunch of street urchins and ragamuffins?"

"You'd be surprised what we can do," Wiggins replied loftily.

"Yes, I'm sure I would. How many of you are there?"

"Seven."

"But we got lots and lots of friends," Beaver interjected. "And we can go everywhere. Nobody notices us, 'cos they don't think we're worth botherin' with."

"They think we're just a bunch of street urchins and ragamuffins," added Wiggins with a sly grin.

The man paused, thinking hard. Then he shook his head. "I don't think so," he said at last. "It would be far too dangerous."

"Never mind that," said Beaver. "We're used to danger. Fenian terrorists, Black Hand gang assassins, Indian thugs, Chinese triads. We seen 'em all off."

"Course," Wiggins continued, "we could just tell Madame Dupont and the police how you broke in here in the middle of the night, like a burglar..."

"You could. But who'd believe you? A bunch of street urchins..."

"Madame Dupont would. And PC Higgins – he knows us. And Inspector Lestrade of Scotland Yard. And then there's Mr Holmes…"

"Enough, enough! Very well, you may help me. But there is one condition. You must not breathe a word of this to anyone – not Madame and certainly not your police friends – until the matter is settled. Do you agree?"

"Hold on," said Wiggins. "We ain't agreed to take the case yet. We don't know who you are, or what it's all about. Right, Beav?"

"Right." Beaver stared suspiciously at the man, and then indicated the wax model. "For a start, if you ain't him, who are you?"

"My name is Selwyn Murray. He was my twin brother, Alwyn."

"Twins! No wonder you look exac'ly the same."

"Not exactly. We are – were – what they call mirror twins. Everything was the same, but the other way round. I have a mole on my left cheek, for instance, Alwyn had one on his right, and so on. I am right-handed, Alwyn was left-handed."

"Oh, I get you," said Beaver. "Just like lookin' at yourself in a mirror."

"Precisely."

"Well, in that case," said Wiggins, shining his lantern on the wax figure once again, "Madame D got it wrong. Look, he's got the gun in his *right* hand."

"A natural mistake, you might think."

"Yeah – 'cept it weren't her mistake."

"How d'you mean?" asked Beaver, puzzled.

Selwyn Murray looked acutely at Wiggins. "Go on," he said.

Wiggins moved over to the photographs and tapped one of them meaningfully. "Look at this picture, where he's shot hisself and he's lying 'cross the desk, dead."

"Do I have to?" Beaver asked with a little groan.

"See where the gun is?"

"Oh, yeah – it's by his right hand!"

"Exac'ly! If he'd shot hisself, he'd have used his left hand, and that's where the gun would have dropped."

"Hmm. You're a clever lad to have spotted

that," said Selwyn Murray. "Maybe you will be able to help me after all."

"Course we will. It's plain to me that there's been some jiggery-pokery going on here."

"That's precisely what I believe. Someone arranged this so that the world would think my poor brother killed his wife and child, then took his own life."

"You mean somebody else murdered them all?" gasped Beaver.

Murray nodded grimly.

"Why'd they do that?" Wiggins asked him.

"Because," he said, "they thought Alwyn was me."

Sarge opened the door of his lodge cautiously and peered out through the narrow crack.

"It's us," whispered Wiggins. "Beaver and me."

"Are you all right?" Sarge opened the door wider, then stopped as he glimpsed a shadowy figure behind them in the darkness. "Who's that?"

"We found your ghost. Only it ain't his ghost, it's his twin."

"What you talking about?"

"Let us in, quick, and I'll tell you."

Sarge stood back and watched suspiciously as the dark-haired man followed the two Boys into the lodge. And although he had been warned, he still caught his breath as the light fell on Selwyn Murray's face.

"It's him!" he exclaimed. "He's the one I saw."

"That's right, Sarge," said Wiggins. "This is Mr Selwyn Murray, twin brother of Mr Alwyn Murray, deceased. He ain't no ghost."

"So you wasn't drunk," added Beaver.

"Not at first, anyway," Wiggins said with a grin.

"Well, I'm blowed." Sarge puffed out his cheeks and collapsed into a chair.

"I believe I owe you an apology, Sergeant." Murray bowed his head to him. "I am very sorry to have caused you so much trouble."

"*Trouble?* You scared me half out of my mind last night!"

"I really didn't mean to. And I shall do everything in my power to make things right again."

"Hmph," Sarge snorted. "That's somethin', I suppose. What was you doin' in there anyhow?"

"Visiting my brother – and looking for clues to his death."

"Couldn't you have done that durin' openin' hours, like any normal person, 'stead of creepin' about in the middle of the night pretendin' to be a ghost? All you had to do was come and ask."

Murray shook his head. "I might have been seen."

"You *was* – by me. And a real nasty turn you give me, I can tell you!"

"There are people who want me dead. At the moment they cannot be sure that I am back in London, but I know they will be watching for me, waiting to kill me as they killed my brother."

"But your brother done hisself in," Sarge said. "After he'd killed his missus and their poor little girl."

"No, he didn't," Wiggins said.

"How d'you know that?"

"'Cos he was a mirror twin," Beaver explained. "So everythin' was the other way round, only they didn't know that, so they put the gun in his wrong hand, and Madame Dupont didn't know that either, so she copied the photos and…"

"Steady on!" Sarge cried, utterly confused. "Hold your horses. You've lost me."

"Perhaps it would be better if I were to explain," said Murray.

"I wish you would."

"My brother did not kill himself, or his wife and child. They were all brutally murdered."

"Whatever would anybody want to do that for?" Sarge asked, shocked.

"Because they thought he was me."

"You mean whoever it was wanted to kill *you*? Why?"

"Because I know too much."

Sarge shook his head in bewilderment. "I'd better put the kettle on," he said. "I think I'm goin' to need a strong cup of tea."

DANGLING THE BAIT

Sarge filled his kettle with water and put it on his little gas ring to heat up. While they waited for it to boil, Murray began his story.

"First," he said to Sarge, "I must swear you to secrecy. Unless anything happens to me, you must tell no one about this – or about me. These boys have already agreed. I am only telling you because I have caused you so much trouble already and I want you to know why. I will do all I can to put things right, but you will have to be patient."

"I suppose I can wait till Lord Holdhurst gets back next week," Sarge replied grudgingly. "That's when I'll get the sack."

"I won't let that happen, I promise."

"All right, then. Your secret's safe with me – till next week."

"Good. Because it is not just my life that is in danger, but the security of our country."

When he heard that, Sarge stood to attention and raised his hand in a smart salute. "I'm an old soldier, sir," he said. "You can rely on me to do my patriotic duty."

"And us," said Beaver, copying him.

"Hang on," Wiggins interrupted. "Your brother was killed months ago. If it's that important, how come it's took you so long to do anything about it?"

"I have only just found out. I've been away – far away – and out of touch."

"Why? Where've you been?"

Murray hesitated, a troubled expression on his face. "I can't tell you that," he said.

Wiggins looked steadily at him, then slowly shook his head. "Well, if you don't trust us," he said, "I don't see how we can help you."

"It's not that I don't trust you. But if I told you, it might put your lives in danger. I don't know if I'm prepared to take that responsibility."

"We don't mind a bit of danger, do we Beav?"

"Er, no," said Beaver, sounding a bit less sure,

but ready as always to follow wherever Wiggins led. "We're used to it."

"Very well. I have been in a Russian prison camp."

"Cor!" exclaimed Beaver. "What was you doin' in Russia? You a spy or somethin'?"

"Something like that," Murray admitted. "I was trying to recover some secret plans that had been stolen from the British Admiralty."

"And the Russkis caught you?"

"Yes. Someone betrayed me."

"You was lucky they didn't shoot you," said Sarge. "That's what they usually do to spies, ain't it?"

"I suppose they thought I might be of more use to them alive than dead. So they locked me away in the frozen wastes of Siberia. I managed to escape, but I was a thousand miles from any-where and being hunted by the secret police. It's taken me months to make my way home."

"And when you got here, you discovered that your brother was dead," said Beaver. "That must have been terrible."

"Yes, it was," said Murray, biting his lip at

the memory. "It was a terrible blow, made even worse by knowing that it should have been me."

"But if you was working for the government, why don't you go to the police?" Wiggins asked.

Murray gave a bitter laugh. "Because that would let them know that I am alive and back in this country. It was someone from our government who betrayed me to the Russians."

"A traitor!" Wiggins exclaimed.

"That's what I discovered in Russia – that there is a traitor high up in the British Admiralty. And I know that he and his associates want me dead before I can unmask him. They will stop at nothing to prevent me from doing so."

"Do you know who the traitor is?" asked Beaver.

"Not for sure. I suspect two or three people, but until I have proof, I daren't show myself. If I were wrong, I would have alerted the real villain – and then I'd be done for."

"There must be somebody you can trust," said Sarge.

"No," said Murray despondently, his shoulders sagging. "Whoever I go to may turn out to be the traitor, or somebody in league with him.

There is no one."

"Hang on," Wiggins said, "there *is* somebody. You got the Baker Street Boys."

Murray lifted his head and smiled. "So I have," he agreed.

"I told you we'll help you. Now, first things first – where are you staying?"

"I've taken a room in a cheap lodging house not far from here, somewhere they wouldn't think of looking."

"But they might – and somebody might spot you coming and going. That won't do. We gotta keep you out of sight while we get to work. And it's gotta be somewhere where we can report back to you without nobody noticing us."

"What about HQ?" suggested Beaver. "He could have my bed. I don't mind."

"You're a good lad, Beav," Wiggins told him, "but I don't think he'd be very comfortable. I got a better idea."

"What's that?"

"You got an empty shop at the far end of the Bazaar, ain't you, Sarge?"

The commissionaire nodded enthusiastically –

he was starting to enjoy this real-life spy adventure.

"That's right," he said. "We haven't been able to find a new tenant since old Mrs Pettigrew died. She used to sell ribbons and embroidery threads and such. The windows are boarded up, so nobody can see in. It'd make a perfect hideout."

"That sounds splendid," said Murray. "I could camp out there and no one would know."

"There's even a few bits of furniture," added Sarge. "Old Ma P had a couch in the back room so she could lie down when she felt poorly, which she often did. You'll be right as rain, sir. The lads could bring you provisions, and I'd be here on sentry duty."

"Excellent. Couldn't be better." Murray's eyes sparkled with fresh life and he straightened his back, cheered by the prospect of doing something positive. "We must start planning our campaign immediately."

It was already getting light by the time Wiggins and Beaver got back to HQ. They woke up the other Boys, who tumbled out of their beds and crowded around them, eager to know what had happened.

"Did you see it?" Rosie asked eagerly. "Did you see the ghost?"

"Well, we did and we didn't..." Wiggins replied.

"That's plain silly," scoffed Shiner. "Don't you know?"

"Yes, we do," Beaver retorted. "We did see what Sarge *thought* was a ghost ..."

"...only it wasn't," Wiggins continued. "It was a real live geezer, what looks exac'ly like the dead bloke in the waxworks,"

"On account of him being his twin mirror," added Beaver.

"His what?" asked Queenie. "I ain't never heard of anybody bein' a lookin'-glass."

"His mirror-twin brother," Wiggins corrected, going on to explain what it meant and how it proved that Alwyn had been murdered. Then he told them the whole story, and how and why Selwyn was in danger. "But we're gonna help him," he concluded. "We're gonna catch the traitor and the murderer."

"Sounds dangerous," observed Shiner.

"That's never stopped us afore," Sparrow said scornfully. "Sounds excitin' to me."

"And me," Gertie agreed. "An excitin' adventure. Can't wait."

"Half a mo'," said Queenie. "What about poor old Sarge? Ain't we supposed to be gettin' him his job back?"

"We will," Wiggins assured her. "Soon as it's safe for Mr Murray to show hisself."

"Anyway," Beaver added, "Sarge knows all about it. He's in on it too."

"I s'pose that's all right, then. So, what do we have to do?"

Wiggins took off his billycock hat and produced two envelopes from inside it. He smoothed them out and laid them carefully down on the table. Above the name and address on each of them were written the words PRIVATE AND CONFIDENTIAL in bold letters.

"First thing we gotta do is deliver these," he said.

"What are they?" Rosie asked.

"Bait."

"You mean like on a fishin' line?" said Gertie.

"Exac'ly," grinned Wiggins. "And we're gonna catch a big fish. Mr Murray reckons the traitor's one of two men, but he don't know which one.

So he's wrote these letters as bait. Now we gotta dangle the bait and see which of 'em takes it."

"Then what do we do?" asked Shiner.

"We keep an eye on him, and report everything we see to Mr Murray at the Bazaar. He'll tell us what to do next."

After they had eaten a hurried breakfast, Wiggins divided the Boys into two groups of three – Queenie, Shiner and Gertie in one; Beaver, Rosie and Sparrow in the other. He read out the two names and addresses on the envelopes and told each group which one to watch. The two houses were in different districts, though not too far apart, and both were in fairly easy walking distance from Baker Street.

"Shouldn't be too hard," he said. "All you gotta do is wait for your man to come out, then track him."

"Yeah, but how will we know who to track?" Queenie asked. "I mean, we don't know what either of 'em looks like."

"That's right," agreed Beaver. "I mean, if some other geezer comes out of the house first, we might follow him and that'd be no good 'cos he'd be the wrong geezer – and if we was to do that, then the geezer we was supposed to be followin' would come out later and we wouldn't be there to follow him, 'cos we'd be busy followin'—"

"Right! Right," Wiggins interrupted him. "Good point. But I've already thought of that." `

He paused, thinking hurriedly while the others watched him and waited for him to go on.

"Well?" Shiner prompted suspiciously.

"Well, what we do is this..." Wiggins replied slowly. Then his face cleared and he went on confidently, as though he had known the answer all along. "When we gets to each house, I go up to the front door and ring the bell. Then when somebody opens it, I say I got a message for the bloke whose name's on the envelope and I gotta give it to him personal. I say I been told it's urgent and I'm not to hand it to nobody else. And when they fetch him to the door, I get him to come right out onto the doorstep so you can have a good gander at him."

"But that means he'll get a good gander at you," said Beaver. "And if he gets a good gander at you, he'll know you and if—"

"Don't matter," said Wiggins, quickly cutting him off. "He won't have seen the rest of you, and you'll be the ones following him."

"Cor." Sparrow gazed at Wiggins admiringly. "That's brilliant. You think of everythin', don't you."

"I try. Now come on, let's get going!"

The first address was in a quiet street in Mayfair, the most expensive area in all London. While the others stood back, trying to look as though they were nothing to do with him, Wiggins walked up to the shiny black front door and pulled the highly polished brass bell handle.

"I got a letter for Sir Charles White," he told the manservant who opened the door.

The man regarded him with disdain and said nothing but held out a white-gloved hand. Wiggins shook his head and told him he had strict instructions not to give the letter to anyone but Sir Charles in person. The man glared at Wiggins through hard, pale eyes set deep under a heavy brow. He was a big, burly man who towered over the leader of the Baker Street Boys, and for a moment Wiggins thought he might seize the letter. He stepped back out of reach.

"Wait there," the man rasped, and he disappeared back into the house, closing the door carefully behind him to make sure Wiggins didn't follow.

It was a full two minutes before the manservant opened the door again. He stood holding it for a distinguished-looking gentleman in a black frock-coat and grey striped trousers, who inspected Wiggins carefully.

"I understand you have something for me," he said.

"Are you Sir Charles White?" Wiggins asked him, stepping back from the doorway.

"I am he."

"Can you prove it?"

"Don't be impertinent, boy! Hand it over."

"Only, the bloke what give it to me made me promise I wouldn't give it to nobody except Sir Charles White."

"Hmm. Who is this 'bloke', may I ask?"

"I dunno, guv. Foreign-looking geezer. He come up to me in the street and give me a bob to bring this to you. That's all I know about him."

"Gave you a shilling, eh? An expensive delivery when he could have popped it in a post box for a penny."

"Yes, guv. Must be something special, eh?"

"We shall see. Give the boy sixpence, will you, Fredericks?" He stepped out of the door to take the letter from Wiggins's hand as the servant scowled and delved into his pocket to find a coin. "Thank you. You can run along now."

Happy that the Boys had had a good look at Sir Charles, Wiggins posted Beaver, Rosie and Sparrow on watch and left with the others for the next address.

This turned out to be a much smaller house, in a shabby road on the other side of busy Oxford Street. The familiar cheerful oom-pahs of a German band greeted the Boys, and Gertie pointed as the musicians approached.

"Sure and isn't that the band that was playin' outside the Bazaar when we found Sarge?" she asked.

"You're right," Wiggins replied. "They do get around, don't they!"

He took the second envelope out of his hat, checked the address and pointed to a front door across the street. The brown paint was beginning to peel, the brass doorknocker was dull for want of polish, and the whole house looked slightly neglected.

"What a mess," Queenie sniffed, remembering her time at Mountjoy House. "Mrs Ford would never stand for that – she'd have the servants on to it in no time."

"You gonna show 'em how it's done, sis?" Shiner teased her.

"You could apply for the housekeeper's job, now you're an expert," Gertie joined in.

"We'll have less of your cheek, if you don't mind," retorted Queenie, giving her a playful cuff around the ear.

Wiggins began to cross the road to the house, but he was barely halfway there when the door opened and a man came out, blinking at the morning light through steel-rimmed glasses. Although, like Sir Charles, he was dressed in the black coat and striped trousers of a government official, there was something distracted about him. His coat was crumpled, the creases down the front of his trousers were not really sharp, and his shoes were scuffed. His leather dispatch case looked worn, his umbrella was not as tightly rolled as it should have been, and wisps of hair protruded untidily from beneath his bowler hat.

"D'you think that's him?" whispered Queenie.

"Gotta be," said Wiggins. "Split up, quick!"

He hurried after the man, who was setting off in the direction of Oxford Street, and quickly caught up with him.

"Beg pardon, sir," he called out as he drew level. "Would you be Mr Harold Redman?"

"I am he. Why?"

Wiggins handed over the letter and gave the same story that he had given Sir Charles. Redman looked puzzled, but thanked him and tore open the letter at once. As he read it, he became agitated.

"Bad news, guv?" Wiggins asked innocently.

"Er, no… No…" He fished his watch out of his waistcoat pocket and consulted it, looking worried and distant. Suddenly remembering Wiggins, he handed him a sixpence, thanked him and set off at a brisk pace.

Wiggins signalled to the others, and the four of them followed Redman along the street, dodging between cabs and carriages and omnibuses as he threaded his way over Oxford Street and into Soho Square. He hurried across the garden in the middle of the square, past the little black-and-white pavilion at its centre, and out onto one of the narrow streets that led from it. Soho was one of the oldest areas of London, popular with immigrants and refugees from France, Italy and a host of other countries. So many of them had opened restaurants and shops selling food and other goods from their own countries that the Boys felt they could easily have been in a foreign land.

Redman's pace did not slacken until he reached his goal, which turned out to be a café in a quiet side street. A bell jangled as he pushed his way through the door. It was hard to see inside through the heavy lace curtains that hung at the window, and in any case the glass was steamed up. Queenie looked up and saw the café's name painted above it. She pointed to it. LUBA's, the sign read, and underneath: RUSSIAN TEA ROOM.

"Bingo!" said Wiggins.

RUSSIAN TEA AND BLINI

The Mayfair street was quiet. Too quiet for Beaver, Rosie and Sparrow, who were afraid they would be noticed while they watched and waited for Sir Charles to make a move. But when the black front door finally opened, it was the tough-looking manservant, Fredericks, who emerged. He stood on the edge of the pavement, looked up and down the road impatiently, then walked quickly away.

"What d'you reckon?" Beaver asked the other two. "Should we follow him?"

"He could be on a secret mission for his boss," Rosie suggested.

"That's right," said Sparrow. "He could be his henchman what he sends to do his dirty work."

"You go after him," Rosie said. "Me and

Sparrow will stop here and keep an eye open for Sir Charlie."

"Watch out for yourself, though," warned Sparrow. "He looks like he could turn nasty."

Beaver ambled off down the street and round the corner behind Fredericks, trying to look as though he was not actually following him, while Rosie and Sparrow settled down again to watch and wait. In the next street the manservant hailed a hansom cab and climbed into it. To Beaver's surprise, he took the cab straight back to his master's house, then held the door open as Sir Charles came down the steps and climbed in.

"Blimey," said Sparrow. "Must be nice to be rich. Old Charlie don't even have to call a cab for hisself!"

"Yeah," Rosie agreed. "Not when he's got a henchman to do it for him."

"Wonder what else he does for him. We better keep our eyes open." Sparrow turned to Beaver, who had just arrived back. "You stick with Charlie. We'll stop here and keep an eye on Fred."

They didn't have long to wait. The cab was hardly out of sight round the corner with Beaver trotting after it, before Fredericks came out of the house again. He looked carefully up and down the street, then set off at a smart pace, seemingly unaware of his two young shadows.

Outside Luba's Russian Tea Room, Wiggins fished out the sixpences he had just earnt and handed them to Queenie. "You and the others go in and get a cup of tea or something," he told her. "And have a good look around. See what Redman's up to and who he's talking to. I'll keep out of the way in case he sees me and twigs he's being followed."

"Can I 'ave a bun?" Shiner asked.

"Or a piece of toast," Gertie said wistfully. "I'd love a piece of warm toast with loads o' butter and maybe a wee drop of jam like my da used to..."

"Hold on," Wiggins interrupted sternly. "We ain't here to enjoy ourselves. We're here to do a job."

"Right," agreed Queenie. "Come on, you two. See you in a minute, Wiggins. D'you want us to send you out a piece of toast or somethin'?"

Wiggins pulled a sour face at her as she

pushed open the door of the café and went in with Shiner and Gertie. They were met with a thick fug of steam from a giant silver urn on the counter and clouds of sharp-smelling smoke from the cigars, pipes and cigarettes that many of the customers were puffing at. The place was only half full, but the noise was tremendous. Everyone seemed to be talking at once, gabbling and arguing at the tops of their voices in what sounded like several different languages. Those who weren't talking sat hunched over newspapers printed in a strange alphabet, which not even Queenie could read. The papers were attached to wooden rods with a hook at one end, and more copies hung from a rack by the counter so that people could borrow them to read while they ate and drank.

A bony woman in a black dress with a long white apron tied around her waist was collecting plates and glasses from the tables. Her dark hair was pulled back into a severe bun, and a pair of metal-rimmed glasses was clipped on her nose. She looked at the Boys with suspicion, as though she were expecting them to make trouble, and she blocked their way in, setting her hands akimbo.

"What you want?" she demanded in a thick foreign accent.

"We'd like three cups of tea and some buns, if you please," Queenie answered in her politest voice. "It's all right, we got the money." And she held up the two sixpences.

The woman's lip curled scornfully. She plucked one of the coins from Queenie's hand and pointed at an empty table.

"Sit!" she ordered fiercely. "There! No cup tea, no buns. This Russian tea room. You have glass tea and blini."

"What's berlini?" Queenie asked nervously.

"Blini is little pancakes. Is good. You will like."

The Boys sat down at the glass-topped table as the woman marched across to the counter. While she busied herself preparing their food and drinks, they looked around at the other customers. Two men at a corner table frowned in concentration as they hunched over a chess board. In another corner, Redman was talking urgently to a man with wild hair and an unruly black beard. They were speaking very quietly and glancing nervously round the room. They were clearly talking about the letter Wiggins had delivered, which Redman still held in his hand. Then he put it down on the table, smoothed it out and jabbed at it with his finger. The bearded man wiped his own fingers on his loose red shirt, then picked up the letter and examined it carefully. He shook his head, puzzled. After a few more words, Redman pulled out his watch, then got to his feet, quickly shook the other man's hand and hurried out into the street.

"We gonna follow him?" Gertie asked.

Before Queenie could answer, the waitress arrived back at their table. She set down three saucers on which stood tall glasses in silvery metal holders with curly handles, a large plate piled with small round pancakes, three little plates and finally a bowl of strawberry jam. The glasses were filled with clear, steaming liquid, each with a slice of lemon floating on top.

"Eat! Drink!" she commanded, and she stood watching to make sure they did.

"What's this?" Shiner asked, pointing to the glasses.

"Tea."

"Where's the milk?"

"No milk. Russian tea with lemon. Very good."

"Lemon?" Gertie said. "Sure and that sounds too sour for me."

"You put in sugar," the woman told her, pointing to a glass bowl filled with sugar lumps.

Shiner needed no second bidding. He scooped up a handful of lumps, which he dropped into his glass and stirred with the long spoon from the saucer, then popped another into his mouth, crunching and sucking contentedly. Gertie quickly did the same. Queenie just managed to get the last two lumps before Shiner emptied the entire bowl. The Russian woman shook her head, stern-faced, as Shiner turned to the blini.

"Is good, no? she asked, as he spread jam on the first one and took a bite.

"Mmm," he nodded vigorously, his mouth full. The little pancakes really were delicious, and in no time at all the plate was empty. The woman grunted her unsmiling approval and took it away.

"What we gonna do about…?" Gertie whispered once she had gone, jerking her head towards the door through which Redman had left.

"Wiggins'll pick him up," Queenie whispered back. "We'll keep an eye on that one," she said, nodding towards the bearded man in the corner. Then, to the Boys' delight, the waitress brought them a second plate of blini. Relieved to see that the bearded man in the red shirt was showing no sign of leaving yet, Queenie, Shiner and Gertie tucked in heartily, wondering hopefully how many more platefuls the waitress might bring them before they had to go.

Beaver had no trouble keeping up with Sir Charles's cab. To begin with it was slowed by heavy traffic, and then it was stuck behind a troop of cavalry soldiers, their horses' hooves making a deafening clatter as they walked steadily on. Beaver had no need to run and could enjoy looking at the white plumes bobbing on the Life Guards' tall silver helmets, their breastplates gleaming in the morning sunlight above their scarlet tunics, white breeches and thigh-length black boots. He watched the curved sabres in the soldiers' glittering scabbards swinging from their belts, and he shivered as he imagined them being used against the enemy in a cavalry charge.

Sir Charles's cabbie seemed content to sit behind the Life Guards, and Beaver was content to plod along behind them both, wondering why the cab didn't try to overtake them or turn off. They passed in front of a grand, brown stone building that Beaver recognized as Buckingham Palace, and continued along the Mall through St James's Park until they reached the open space of Horse Guards Parade.

The horses and men of the old guard, who had been on duty since the day before, were lined up on the parade ground waiting, the horses' heads tossing impatiently. As the new guard arrived and lined up to face them, a trumpeter sounded a silvery call and the ceremony of handing over began. Beaver watched, fascinated, as standards changed hands and swords flashed in salute. He imagined how good it would feel to be one of those proud soldiers. He was so fascinated, in fact, that he quite forgot what he was supposed to be doing until he suddenly realized that the cab had gone. He began to panic. What was he to do? He had lost Sir Charles.

Wiggins had ducked into a doorway as Redman came out of the Russian tea room. The man looked anxiously at his watch and set off quickly, almost breaking into a trot as he hurried through the Soho streets past the restaurants, shops and cafés, sometimes having to hop sideways into the road as an owner swished a bucket of water across the pavement to clean it. Wiggins dropped carefully into step a few yards behind, making sure there were always a few people between them but never enough to lose sight of his target altogether.

On they went, leaving Soho behind, then crossing Trafalgar Square. Still Redman hurried on, dodging through the traffic into Whitehall, a broad street filled with government offices, with Wiggins trailing a few yards behind. Finally, he turned off into the courtyard of an elegant red-brick building through a gateway with an anchor built into its arch. Wiggins tried to follow but was stopped by a uniformed marine, who asked where he thought he was going.

"Er, I'm with him," he stammered, pointing to Redman's retreating back as he disappeared into the building.

"A likely tale, I don't think," the marine scoffed. "On yer way, sunshine."

Wiggins shrugged. There was clearly no point in trying to argue. "What is this place, anyway?" he asked.

"Don't you know nothing?" the marine replied. "This is the Admiralty. Her Majesty's Board of Admiralty, if you want the proper title."

"And what goes on here?"

"Goes on?" The man stared at Wiggins as though he were an idiot. "Why, this is where they run the Royal Navy."

Wiggins sniffed and pretended to look around. "Where's all the ships, then?" he asked cheekily. He peered past the sailor, as though looking for ships. He didn't see any, of course. What he did see, however, was the back of a man standing in a tall first-floor window, consulting his watch. A moment later another man appeared beside him, looking flustered and apologetic. It was Redman. As the first man turned to greet him, Wiggins caught sight of his face and his jaw dropped. Sir Charles.

In an instant, the two men had disappeared from sight inside the building. Wiggins stood wondering about what he had seen. Were they in cahoots? Could it be that they were both guilty? That *both* were spies and traitors?

Wiggins was brought back to earth by the sentry, who asked what the matter was. "You look like you seen a ghost or something," he said.

"Something like that, yeah," Wiggins replied distractedly. He moved off down the street, away from the marine's gaze. A few yards further on, a mounted Life Guard in full uniform sat motionless on his horse, his drawn sword resting on his right shoulder. A small crowd of visitors to London stood looking at him. Among them, to Wiggins's surprise, was Beaver.

"What you doing here?" he asked.

Beaver hung his head in shame. "Sorry, Wiggins," he confessed. "I lost Sir Charles."

Wiggins shook his head slowly and tutted,

unable to resist teasing Beaver. "That was very careless of you, Beav," he reproached him. "Guess what, though? It's OK – I just found him."

Outside the Mayfair house, Rosie was wishing she had brought her tray of flowers with her. It would have given her something to do, and she might have earnt a few pennies, too. Sparrow passed the time by practising card tricks with the pack he always carried in his pocket. He was halfway through trying to produce four aces from nowhere, when the shiny black door opened again and Fredericks came out, now wearing a square bowler hat and a short coat. As he marched off down the street, Sparrow nodded to Rosie, scooped up his cards and set off after him. Rosie followed on the other side of the street.

Fredericks crossed Park Lane into Hyde Park and took one of the many footpaths towards the Serpentine, the big lake in the middle of the park. Without pausing, he strode past nursemaids with children and older people enjoying a gentle morning stroll along the bank. Unlike them, he obviously had a purpose in mind, and the two

Boys found it hard to keep up without running. The manservant finally slowed down as he reached the embankment carrying the main road through the park onto a long stone bridge across the water. The footpath continued under the road, through a narrow, arched tunnel in the embankment. After looking carefully around him, Fredericks slipped into this tunnel – and out of sight.

Sparrow didn't dare follow him into the tunnel – he would be too easily seen. Instead, he hurried up the bank, crossed the road and waited for Fredericks to come out on the other side. But to his surprise there was no sign of the tough manservant. Could it be, he wondered, that there was a secret passage down there? After a few minutes, he gave up and began to cross back over the road – only to see the man reappear, heading up the slope to the parapet of the bridge. Ducking behind a bush, Sparrow watched, intrigued, as Fredericks seemed to lean against the parapet for a moment, then turned and marched back the way he had come.

Sparrow scuttled across the road to rejoin Rosie. "What do we do now?" he asked. "Follow him, or wait till he's out of sight, then go under the bridge to see what he was up to?"

"Let's wait. He looks like he's goin' home."

"'Spect you're right," Sparrow said. "Job done, eh?"

"Yeah. But we gotta try and find out what that job was. And what he was doin' when he was up there on top. Looked like he was writing somethin' with a piece of chalk."

"Did it? I couldn't see – he had his back to me. Let's take a look."

Waiting until they were sure Fredericks had gone, Sparrow and Rosie clambered up the bank to the roadway. Sure enough, where he had been standing, something was chalked on the flat top of the parapet. It looked like two "V"s – or perhaps a "W".

"V V? W?" Sparrow said, puzzled. "What's that mean?"

"Wait a minute!" exclaimed Rosie. "Look at it the other way up."

"The other way... Oh, my word! It ain't a 'W' – it's an 'M'!"

"Right. 'M' for Moriarty!"

A DEAD-LETTER DROP

Sparrow and Rosie scrambled down the bank from the road and into the shadowy tunnel underneath. It was quite empty and they could see nothing that looked at all suspicious – no alcoves or gratings or doors that might have led to a secret chamber or passageway. Only plain stone walls.

"Don't look like many people come through here," Sparrow said, looking at the moss growing on the footpath.

"You can see where he walked," said Rosie, pointing to where Fredericks's feet had flattened it. The footprints showed that he couldn't have gone far under the bridge before he had stopped and faced the wall.

"Beats me what he was up to," said Sparrow, scratching his head.

"Yeah," Rosie agreed. "Hold on, though. Take a dekko at this." Crouching down to get a closer look, she pointed to a little pile of pale dust on the ground. She took a pinch of it in her fingers and showed it to Sparrow. "What d'you think that is?"

"Mortar," he said, examining it. Then he looked at the wall above. "Hello. What we got here, then? This bit looks like it's loose."

The joint between two of the stones, which Sparrow was looking at, was about three feet above the ground. The edges of the strip of mortar between them stood out very slightly, and he got his fingers around it and wiggled until he could get a proper hold and ease it out. He laid it down on the ground and poked his fingers into the gap where it had been.

"What you found?" asked Rosie impatiently.

"There's a space been hollowed out behind. And there's somethin' hid there."

"Let's see, let's see!"

After a bit of scrabbling around with his fingers, Sparrow eventually pulled out a slim package wrapped in waterproof cloth. He laid it gently on the ground and unfolded it to reveal a sealed envelope.

"It's a letter," he said excitedly. "A secret message!"

"Now then, lads!" Sarge greeted Wiggins and Beaver as they arrived at his lodge. "Back from patrol, are you?"

"Yes, Sarge. We've come to report."

"Right. Fall in, then!"

"Fall in what?" asked Beaver, puzzled.

"No, no! Not *in* anything. Get fell in!"

"He means line up," Wiggins explained, "like being on parade. It's what they says in the army."

"No talkin' in the ranks!" Sarge barked. "Stand to attention, there!"

"Sarge," Wiggins interrupted, "we're on a secret mission. We don't want nobody seeing us report to Mr Murray."

"That's right," added Beaver in a low voice. "It's very hush-hush."

"Ah. Yes. I was forgettin' that. Fall out. You'd better sneak through the Bazaar and go to him."

"Yes, Sarge."

"And try to make sure nobody sees you."

"Nobody sees you doing what?" asked a familiar voice behind them. Dr Watson was standing in the doorway of the lodge, regarding them curiously.

"Doctor!" exclaimed Wiggins, wondering how much he had heard. "What you doing here?"

"I might ask you the same question. I was passing by and thought I'd call in to see my old comrade Sergeant Scroggs."

"Well, fancy that," said Wiggins. "That's just what we're doing!"

"We've come to report— Ow!" Beaver stopped with a yelp as Wiggins kicked his ankle.

"Report?" Dr Watson asked.

"Report for duty," Wiggins said quickly. "To see if there's any jobs need doing around the Bazaar. Anything we can help Sarge with."

"That's very thoughtful of you," said the doctor.

"Oh, yes, sir," said Sarge. "They're good lads. Don't know what I'd do without 'em."

"Yes, Mr Holmes often says that." Dr Watson smiled at the two Boys. "I don't suppose you've managed to persuade Madame Dupont to change her mind and withdraw her complaint?"

"No, sir," Wiggins replied. "Not yet."

"But we're workin' on it," said Beaver. "Now we know Sarge wasn't seein' things, and that he wasn't drunk."

"You may *know* it, but can you prove it?"

"We can, sir," Wiggins told him. "And we will. But we're sworn to secrecy."

"Are you indeed?" Dr Watson raised his eyebrows in surprise.

"Yes, sir. Matter of national security," Sarge explained.

"Matter of life and death," Beaver added dramatically.

"Well, I'm dashed. Ghosts and state secrets and matters of life and death…" Dr Watson stared at them doubtfully. "Are you quite sure about all this?"

Before Wiggins could say any more, there was the sound of running footsteps and Rosie and Sparrow arrived, hot and out of breath.

"Wiggins!" Sparrow gasped. "We found a message – a secret message!"

"Sir Charlie's henchman left it under the bridge," Rosie panted. "For Moriarty!"

"Moriarty!" Dr Watson exclaimed. "What is that evil genius involved in now?"

"Dunno, Doctor," Wiggins shrugged, trying to put him off. "First I've heard of it."

"But it's true!" Rosie insisted, oblivious to Wiggins's warning look. "Ain't that right, Sparrow?"

"As I live and breathe," said Sparrow. "And here's the message, to prove it."

He pulled the waterproof package from his pocket and held it out to Wiggins, who snatched it from him and tried to tuck it out of sight as quickly as possible.

"I think you'd better tell me exactly what's going on," Dr Watson said, looking worried. "It sounds as though it could be very dangerous."

"But, we promised…" Beaver began.

"Whatever your secret is, you can trust me to keep it. I give you my word."

"That's good enough for me," said Sarge. "You can tell him."

"I may even be able to help you," the doctor added.

And so, with Beaver chipping in a few extra

details, Wiggins quickly explained the situation to Dr Watson, who listened very carefully, then blew out his cheeks with a low whistle.

"My word," he said. "If this is true…"

"Course it's true!" Wiggins protested.

"Forgive me. I didn't mean to doubt you, my dear Wiggins."

"Good. You'd best come and meet Mr Murray and let him tell you hisself. We gotta give him this letter anyway."

With Sarge keeping watch, Wiggins led the other three Boys and Dr Watson through the Bazaar to Mrs Pettigrew's boarded-up shop. He gave three short knocks on the door followed by another two, the signal they had agreed with Mr Murray, who let them in and closed the door quickly behind them.

"I thought you promised not to tell anybody," Mr Murray admonished when he saw the doctor.

"This ain't just anybody," Wiggins replied. "This is Dr Watson. He works with Mr Holmes."

Murray's face cleared. "Mr Sherlock Holmes?" he asked. "Then you are welcome, Doctor. I presume the Boys have told you about my situation?"

"They have. It is a great pity Holmes is not here. He would have relished a case like yours. I shall do my best to contact him, but when he is working under cover he is almost impossible to locate."

"That is as it should be," said Murray. "In the meantime, it seems the Baker Street Boys have something to report." He turned to Rosie and Sparrow, who were bouncing up and down with impatience. "Yes?"

"Yes!" Rosie cried. "We found a secret message!"

"What Sir Charles's henchman hid!" Sparrow added. "Show him, Wiggins."

Wiggins pulled the letter from his pocket and handed it to Murray, who unwrapped the waterproof cloth and examined the envelope carefully.

"There is no name or address written on it. And it's firmly sealed. You haven't tried to open this?" he asked.

Rosie and Sparrow shook their heads.

"Good. We shall need a little steam. Fortunately, I was about to make myself a cup of tea, so we're halfway there already." He pointed to a kettle which was heating up on a small spirit stove in a corner of the shop. "As you can see, the good Sergeant Scroggs has provided me with a few home comforts. Now, while we are waiting for the water to boil, tell me how you found this letter."

Rosie and Sparrow recounted all that had happened, and how they had seen Fredericks chalking a mark on the bridge and then discovered the hiding place.

"Well done!" said Murray. "That's what is known as a dead-letter drop. A hiding place where a secret agent can leave or pick up messages without risking being seen meeting the other person. The chalk mark would be a sign that there is a message waiting to be collected."

"That's devilish clever, and no mistake!" exclaimed Dr Watson. Then he turned to Rosie and Sparrow, puzzled. "But how could you know it was for Moriarty?"

"Because the sign that Fredericks chalked on the bridge was a letter 'M'," said Rosie.

"'M' for Moriarty!" cried Wiggins. "Of course! Well done."

"Who or what is Moriarty?" asked Murray.

"Professor Moriarty is an evil genius," replied Dr Watson. "Holmes calls him the Napoleon of crime. He regards him as his most fearsome opponent."

"You have encountered him before?" Murray asked Wiggins.

"We've crossed swords with him a few times."

"And won?"

"Yeah. But he's a slippery customer. Always gets somebody else to do his dirty work so you can't pin nothing on him."

"Perhaps this time it will be different," said Murray. "Now, let's see what Sir Charles has got to say to him."

Steam was now puffing out of the boiling kettle. Murray held the letter over the spout and moved it to and fro.

"What you doin'?" Beaver asked.

"The steam will melt the glue on the envelope, and then we can peel it open without cutting the paper," explained Murray. "D'you see?"

"Be careful you don't scald yourself," Dr Watson warned. "Steam can be dangerous stuff.

Hotter than boiling water, you know."

Murray picked up a knife and slid the blade under the flap of the envelope, working it gently along until he could peel it open. There was a note inside: a single sheet of paper folded once. He unfolded it and read aloud what was written on it: *"Spaniards Sat 3."*

"Spaniards?" asked Wiggins. "I thought it was Russkis we was after."

"So did I," said Murray, frowning deeply. "This is confusing. Three *what* sat *where*?"

"It might be a code," suggested Beaver. "You know, when words mean somethin' different."

"Very possible," Murray agreed. "In which case we're lost without the key or a code book. Unless it's something else. There could be secret writing, perhaps…"

He held the sheet of paper up to the light and looked at it very closely. "No," he sighed. "Not even a watermark."

Next, he held it over the spirit stove. "Let's try a little gentle heat," he murmured, taking care not to scorch the paper. "No, nothing. If he *has* used a secret ink, it is not one that reacts to heat.

I need to examine the surface more closely, to see if there are any tiny scratches from a pen. If only I had a lens…"

"This any help?" asked Wiggins, digging into the inside pocket of his coat and producing his magnifying glass.

"Good heavens," said Murray, impressed. "You really are a detective, aren't you?"

"Mr Holmes give me that," Wiggins said proudly.

Murray peered at the note through the powerful lens, then shook his head and handed it back to Wiggins.

"No," he said. "This paper can tell us nothing more. We must get it back to its hiding place before anyone discovers its absence. Now – Mrs Pettigrew must surely have had some glue here, for doing up parcels…" He rummaged around a bit, found what he was looking for in a drawer in the shop counter, and sealed the envelope again with great care. Then he wrapped it in the waterproof cloth and handed it to Sparrow.

"There," he said. "Now hurry and put this back *exactly* where you found it. It must look as though it has never been touched. Off you go!"

Sparrow and Rosie opened the door a little way, looked cautiously through the crack to make sure no one was watching, then dashed back towards the park.

"I shall leave too," said Dr Watson, "and see if I can locate Holmes. When I do, I shall inform him of your case, and I have no doubt he will wish to take it on."

"Thank you, Doctor," said Murray, holding out his hand gratefully. "But remember – not a word to anyone else."

Watson nodded, shook Murray's hand, then slipped quietly out of the door and hurried away through the Bazaar.

"Now," said Murray, turning back to Wiggins and Beaver, "you have told me about Sir Charles, but what about Redman? Did you deliver my letter to him?"

"We did," Wiggins answered. "I give it to him myself."

"And how did he react?"

"He looked bothered, then he went charging off to a caff in Soho."

"Do you know the name of this caff, er, café?"

"Luba's Russian Tea Room."

"Ha!" exclaimed Murray. "Luba's! I know it. It is a meeting place for Russian exiles."

"What's an exile?" Beaver asked.

"A person who has been forced to leave his own country and live somewhere else," Murray told him.

"Who forces 'em?"

"Their government, their police…"

"Why?"

"Usually because they're dangerous revolutionaries."

"You mean they want to blow things up and kill people?" asked Beaver incredulously.

"Some of them do, yes."

"Oh, crikey," said Wiggins, worried. "I sent Queenie and Gertie and Shiner into that caff."

"It's all right," Murray reassured him. "Those revolutionaries only want to kill people from their own government."

"So they wouldn't want to kill *you*? Or your brother if they thought he was you?"

Murray looked serious for a moment. "Not

unless..." he began, then stopped.

"Not unless what?"

"One of them might – if he wasn't a real revolutionary, but an undercover agent working for the Russian secret police."

"You mean just pretending to be a real revolutionary so he could spy on the others?" said Wiggins.

"Exactly. Such a man would not hesitate to murder anyone who could expose him to the people he was spying on."

"Like Queenie and Shiner and Gertie," said Beaver. "If he sees 'em watching him, he'll think they're gonna blow his cover! And then..."

Wiggins was already on his feet and heading for the door. "C'mon, Beav," he cried. "We gotta get 'em outta there afore it's too late!"

A HORNET'S NEST

Queenie, Shiner and Gertie had already left Luba's Russian Tea Room. The bearded man had sat in his corner for a while, staring at the letter Redman had given him. Then, quite suddenly, he seemed to make up his mind about something. Folding the letter and stuffing it into his pocket, he got to his feet and crossed the room to where a woman sat alone at a table, her rich chestnut-coloured hair falling across her face as she scribbled intensely in a notebook. He leant down, whispered something in her ear and jerked his head towards the door. She looked up, startled, then quickly gathered her papers and followed him out, pulling a black cloak around her shoulders.

Shiner went to stand, ready to dash after them, but Queenie laid her hand on his arm.

"Take it easy, now," she whispered. "We don't want to look like we're followin' 'em."

Trying to look casual, the three Boys drained their glasses, then strolled to the door. As they passed the waitress, she reached out and pinched Shiner's cheek between her finger and thumb.

"You come back soon," she said. "I give you more blini." And she almost smiled.

Blushing deep scarlet, Shiner escaped to the street. Queenie and Gertie couldn't help giggling as they followed him out.

"She's taken a proper shine to you," Queenie teased.

"Taken a shine to Shiner, she has," Gertie added with a chuckle.

Shiner scowled furiously and stared past them at the bearded man and the woman, who were standing in a doorway a few yards away, talking hard. The man looked carefully over his shoulder, then took the letter from his pocket and handed it to the woman, who adjusted her spectacles and read it, then stuffed it into her handbag and hurried off down the street without a backward glance.

"C'mon," whispered Queenie. "Let's see where she takes it."

"What about *him*?" Gertie asked.

"I'll stick with Blackbeard," said Shiner, glad of the chance to be free from their teasing. "You two tail 'er. See you back at HQ."

As the two girls set off after the woman, the man walked back past them. For a moment Shiner was afraid he was going back into the café, but to his relief the man continued along the little street and out into a bigger one beyond.

Shiner trailed after him as he turned under an archway, crossed the busy Shaftesbury Avenue and plunged into another area of small streets and ancient alleyways. When he turned into one of these, Shiner hung back for a few seconds, afraid of being seen, then hurried after him. But suddenly there was no sign of the man – he must have sped up and turned into another street. Wondering what to do next, Shiner was halfway along this road when a strong arm shot out of a narrow passage, grabbed him round the neck and pulled him into the darkness. A rough hand clamped over his mouth to stop him crying out.

"Got you," snarled a deep voice. "Why you spy on me? Who send you?"

After running all the way from Baker Street, Sparrow and Rosie were quite out of breath by the time they got back to the bridge over the Serpentine. There were more people in the park than there had been earlier, and Sparrow had to wait a few minutes before he could enter the tunnel without being seen. Rosie kept a lookout while he slid the letter back into its hiding place and replaced the loose piece of mortar. Then they found a spot under a nearby tree where they could sit on the grass and watch everything.

For what seemed like a long time, all was quiet and peaceful. A few people passed through the tunnel: a young couple strolling arm in arm; a nanny pushing a baby in a large wicker pram and a nurse pushing an old man slumped in a wheelchair; a constable on patrol from the nearby police station; two elegant ladies carrying parasols and walking a fluffy white poodle on a lead. None of them seemed at all like spies. Then Rosie spotted something that made her sit up.

"Look!" she cried, pointing up at the bridge.

Sparrow looked – and saw it too. A familiar black carriage had stopped on the roadway above the tunnel.

"It's him!" he gasped. "Moriarty!"

They scrambled to their feet, but before they could even start to run up the bank, the coach-man had whipped up the horse, and the carriage had sped away. By the time the two Boys reached the roadway, it was completely out of sight. They both knew they had no chance of catching it, and they turned back, feeling desolate. Rosie stopped to look at the chalk mark on the parapet.

"Somebody's rubbed it out!" she cried.

"D'you think that means…?" Sparrow began.

"Dunno. Let's go and see."

They careered back down the bank and into the tunnel. Sparrow ran to the loose piece of mortar and eased it out. He poked his fingers into the hole and felt about. There was nothing there – the message had gone.

The woman from the tea room strode through the streets, her black cloak billowing out behind her, clutching her notebook and papers under her arm.

Queenie and Gertie had no difficulty following her – because she was tall, they could easily see her flowing chestnut hair above the heads of the other people, even when the street became quite crowded. After a short distance, she turned off into a quieter road and entered a tall block of flats. Through the glass of the door, they could see a uniformed hall porter greet her with a smart salute. Everything looked extremely respectable.

"D'you think that's where she lives?" Gertie asked.

"Looks like it," Queenie answered. "And there ain't no way we'd get past that doorman. We'll just have to hang about and keep our eyes open."

"Oh, not again," Gertie groaned. "Watch and wait – that's all we ever seem to do on this case."

"Ain't much else we can do for now."

"I know. But it's not very excitin', is it?"

They had not been watching and waiting for very long, however, when the woman came out again, still carrying her notebook. As they followed her this time, she strode back along the busy street, then went into the post office. Leaving Gertie on guard outside, Queenie pushed through the heavy swing doors and found herself among lines of people waiting to hand over letters and parcels to the clerks behind the long counter. At first she could not see the woman, but then she spotted her standing at a separate counter under a sign that said TELEGRAMS AND TELEGRAPHS. She was writing a message on a form, which she handed to the clerk, who read it quickly, counted the number of words and held out her hand for payment. Queenie wished she could see who the telegram was for, but she couldn't get close enough to look. Then she had to duck behind a line of people to keep out of sight as the woman turned from the counter and left the post office.

Outside, Queenie signalled to Gertie and they both began tailing the woman again. She led them round the corner, past several rows of bookshops, to a huge stone building set back from the road behind high black railings. The two girls watched as she walked up the steps leading to the entrance and in through the great wooden doors.

"Cor!" said Gertie, staring up in awe at the enormous stone pillars supporting a great portico filled with classical carvings. "What sort o' place is that?"

Queenie thought it looked like the picture of an ancient Greek or Roman temple which she remembered seeing in one of her mother's books, but the sign on the railings said THE BRITISH MUSEUM. "I've heard of that," she said.

"Museum?" Gertie queried. "Now what on earth could she want in there?"

"Dunno. Let's go and find out."

"They'll never let you and me in, will they?"

"Don't see why not," said Queenie, pointing at a small group of schoolchildren who were following their teacher up the steps. "Come on."

They scurried across the forecourt, tagged on behind the children and soon found themselves inside the museum. Their mouths dropped open as they looked around them at the amazing objects on display. Straight in front was a white stone statue of a helmeted Greek warrior brandishing a sword and shield. To one side stood an Egyptian mummy in a brightly painted sarcophagus. Gold cups and plates gleamed and glistened in a glass-fronted showcase. Queenie would have loved to stop and look at everything properly, but they could see their woman disappearing round a corner and had to hurry after her.

The woman clearly knew exactly where she was going, and she marched on with barely a glance at the wonders all around. Queenie and Gertie just about managed to keep pace with her as she passed by great pieces of marble carved into horses and chariots, and ancient Greek ladies dressed in flowing robes that were so lifelike it was hard to believe they were made of stone.

She eventually halted by a big door and disappeared through it, but when the girls tried to follow, they were stopped by a man in a dark blue uniform and peaked cap.

"You can't go in there," he told them firmly. "Not unless you've got a ticket."

"You mean like a train ticket?" Gertie asked. "Why? Where's it goin' to?"

The man was not amused. "It's not going

anywhere," he said. "That's the Reading Room."

Peeping past him through the glass panels in the door, Queenie could see an enormous, circular room. The walls, right up to the great dome of the roof, were lined with thousands and thousands of books, some of which had to be reached by iron staircases and galleries. Below, dozens of people sat at long desks, curved to fit the shape of the room, reading and writing busily. The woman took her place at one of them, nodding a silent greeting to those nearest to her.

"What they all doin'?" Queenie asked.

"Studying. Thinking. Writing," the attendant told her. "They're very clever people. Scholars and professors and suchlike."

"Will you just look at all 'em books!" gasped Gertie. "I never knew there was so many books in all the world."

The man gave her a superior smile. "We've got a copy of every book that's ever been printed in this country," he said proudly, stroking his heavy moustache. "But they're not for the likes of you. Now hop it, both of you! And don't touch anything on your way out. I'll be watching."

Wiggins and Beaver ran all the way to Soho and arrived, puffing and panting, outside Luba's Russian Tea Room. There was no sign of Queenie, Shiner or Gertie either outside or inside the café, or in any of the streets and alleys near by.

"I'm worried, Beav," Wiggins admitted. "I'll never forgive myself if anything's happened to 'em."

"Don't fret," Beaver tried to reassure him. "There's three of 'em. They'll be OK if they stick together."

"Yeah, I s'pose so. Well, there ain't nothing we can do here now. Better go back to the Bazaar and wait for 'em to show up."

After another quick look around the area, just to make sure, they made their way back to HQ in case the others had returned home and were waiting there for them. But the secret cellar was empty. So, with heavy hearts, they hurried round to the Baker Street Bazaar to report to Murray in his hideout.

They had only just closed the door behind them when there was another knock on it, again in the secret code, and Sparrow and Rosie tumbled breathlessly in.

"It's gone," Rosie gasped. "Somebody's took the message!"

"And now Moriarty's got it," Sparrow added.

"Did you see him?" Wiggins asked. "Did you see Moriarty?"

"No," Rosie admitted, "but we seen his carriage."

"And you didn't follow it?"

"No. He drove off at a good lick. We never had no chance of catchin' it."

"Forget this Moriarty fellow for the moment," Murray cut in impatiently. "Did you see who actually took the message?"

"No," said Rosie. "They was inside the tunnel, see."

"But the only people what went through it all looked respectable," Sparrow added. "None of 'em looked like spies."

"Well, they wouldn't, would they," said Wiggins. "Not if they didn't want nobody to know."

"Quite so," Murray agreed. "But tell me about them, all the same. Describe them to me, if you can remember."

"Course we can remember," Sparrow said scornfully. "We're the Baker Street Boys, ain't we? Mr Holmes learned us what to do."

Between them, Sparrow and Rosie managed to recall and describe all the people they had seen passing through the tunnel in the park. Murray shook his head sadly.

"You're quite right," he said. "It could have been any of them. They all sound perfectly respectable."

"That's how they looked," said Rosie. "There was even a copper."

Murray sat up sharply. "A policeman? You didn't mention him."

"He'd be a park policemen," said Wiggins. "The Royal parks has their own police force, you know."

"I 'spect he was on his way to the police station," said Sparrow. "It's only just round the corner from where we was. He wasn't on duty."

"Why do you say that?" asked Murray.

"He didn't have his armband on. When a copper goes on duty, he puts a striped band on his sleeve, don't he? By his wrist."

"That's correct," agreed Murray. "You're a sharp lad to have spotted that. I'll wager that's our man. He must have collected the message, then handed it over to Moriarty or his coachman."

"Well done, Sparrow," said Wiggins.

"D'you reckon he weren't a proper copper?" Beaver wanted to know.

"You mean somebody pretendin' to be one?" asked Rosie. "Like in disguise?"

"Possibly," Murray replied. "Or a proper copper gone bad. That's why I didn't want to go to the police – I don't know who I can trust."

They were still thinking about this when Queenie and Gertie returned and told them what they had seen in Luba's Russian Tea Room, and how they had trailed the woman.

"She ended up in the British Museum," Queenie said. "Cor! What a place that is. All them carvings and statues and gold and mummies and stuff."

"What was she doing there?" Wiggins asked. "Meeting somebody? Leaving secret messages?"

"No, she went in a sort of library."

"There were millions and millions of books,"

Gertie added. "Sure and I never thought there was that many in the whole wide world!"

"Ah, yes," said Murray. "That'll be the Reading Room. A lot of revolutionaries go there to study and write their own books.

"Is that all she did?" Wiggins asked Queenie.

"No, before the museum, she went to the post office and sent a telegram," Queenie replied. "I couldn't see who it was to, but she looked like it was somethin' urgent."

"Excellent," Murray told her. "We seem to have stirred up a real hornet's nest."

"No, no," said Gertie, "there weren't no hornets. I seen hornets and I don't like 'em. They can sting you somethin' rotten!"

"What's a hornet?" asked Sparrow.

"It's like a wasp, only bigger and nastier," Wiggins said.

"If you get stung by hornets," Beaver added seriously, "you can die."

"Oh dear," cried Rosie. "You don't think...?"

"Hold it!" Wiggins held up his hand. "There ain't no hornets. It's just a saying. Right, Mr Murray?"

"Quite right, Wiggins. If you poke a stick into a hornet's nest, they all come flying out looking for trouble. And that's what our revolutionary friends from Luba's are probably doing."

"Yeah, but what are *we* gonna do now we've stirred 'em up?" asked Sparrow. "I don't much fancy gettin' stung, even if it is only a sayin'."

"Well," said Murray, "now that we're all back together…"

"Hang on," Queenie butted in. "We *ain't* all together, are we? Where's Shiner?"

THE HANGED HIGHWAYMAN

The black-bearded man from the café shoved Shiner into a room and slammed the door shut behind him. The boy heard a key being turned in the lock and then the sound of the man's footsteps clumping across the bare boards of the landing and down the stairs. He hurled himself at the door and hammered on it with his fists, shouting at the top of his voice, "Lemme out! Lemme out!" But the footsteps carried on until another door closed at the foot of the stairs, and then there was silence.

The room seemed to be in the attic of a tall, old house. It was dingy, dusty and dim – the only light seeped in through a small skylight in the ceiling, with glass so grimy it was impossible to tell if the sky above was blue or grey. The only furniture was a single iron bedstead, a rickety wooden chair and a cheap chest of drawers with three legs and a couple of books propping it up where the fourth leg should have been. A large tin trunk sat in one corner of the room, battered and dented from years of use and plastered with old shipping labels.

Shiner looked around desperately for a way of escape, but there was nothing. The skylight was too high for him to reach, even if he stood the chair on top of the trunk or the chest of drawers. And he knew that if he did manage to reach it, he probably wouldn't be able to open it – and even if he got that far it would only lead out onto the steep roof. He worked his way carefully round the bare room, knocking on the walls in the hope that one of them might be hollow – he had heard that in some old buildings the attics and lofts joined up, in which case it might be possible to break through into the house next door. But these walls were all solid.

Angry at himself for allowing Blackbeard to catch him, he let out a scream of rage and kicked at the walls and door until his toes hurt. Then, as his temper cooled, he threw himself down on the bed, wondering fearfully what his captors would do with him. He had no doubts now that he was in the hands of a dangerous gang of revolutionaries. And he had no way of escape.

By the evening, Queenie was starting to get quite worried about her little brother. She knew he could usually take care of himself, but she also knew he often did things that got him into trouble. She wondered if that was why he had not come home for his supper. Even though he had eaten a pile of blini in the tea room, he must be hungry by now – the other Boys were ravenous, and Shiner always had the biggest appetite of them all. Queenie had been too busy to find anything to cook, but Murray had given her some money to buy pies for all of them as well as for himself, and they had taken theirs back to HQ to eat.

When they had finished and Shiner still hadn't returned, Queenie decided she would have to go and look for him.

"I'll come with you," Beaver volunteered. "In case you need backup."

"Me too," said Rosie, jumping up.

"And me," Gertie joined in. "I was with you when he went off after Blackbeard."

"Right," said Queenie. "We can start at the tea room. That's where we last saw him. You comin', Wiggins?"

Wiggins shook his head. "No, I got some thinking to do. 'Sides, somebody oughta stop here, case he comes back while you're out."

Sparrow had already left for his job at the theatre, so once the others had rushed out, Wiggins was alone. He settled down in his special chair to do some hard thinking. He had a nagging feeling at the back of his mind about the strange message, *Spaniards Sat 3*. It was still a puzzle that he couldn't solve, but there was something vaguely familiar about it – he simply couldn't remember what it was. After a while, however, an idea came to him, and he hurried off to see Murray at the Bazaar.

"I bin thinking about your brother," he told him. "You said whoever murdered him did it 'cos they thought he was you."

Murray nodded sadly. "Yes," he said. "It should

have been me. It was my fault he was killed."

"No, it weren't," Wiggins said. "You can't help looking like your twin. But the thing is, if the murderer mistook him for you, he must have seen him somewhere, right?"

"Yes, of course."

"So, if we knew where your brother had been ..."

"...we'd know where the murderer could have been, and that might give us a clue!"

"Exac'ly."

"You're a clever chap, Wiggins, but how do you think we're going to find that out?"

"Well, in Madame Dupont's tableau in the waxworks, your brother is at his desk, right?"

"Right."

"And what's on that desk?"

"Well, the gun, of course..."

"And what else?"

"Pens and ... a book. His diary. By Jove, Wiggins – you could have something there! The diary should tell us what Alwyn had been doing and where he'd been."

"Exac'ly! The waxworks is shut for the night

now, so if I get the key from Sarge, I could nip in there and borrow the diary. We could read it and put it back in the morning, afore they open, and nobody would know."

"Wiggins, my friend, you're more than clever – you're brilliant!"

"Ta very much," said Wiggins with a broad grin.

Queenie, Beaver, Rosie and Gertie peered through the windows of Luba's Russian Tea Room but could see nothing. The café was dark and deserted, with a closed sign hanging inside the door. They stepped back and looked at the upstairs windows, but there were no lights there either. For the next hour, the four Boys combed the streets of Soho, searching every alley and doorway, but they could find no sign of Shiner.

"I'm sure he'll turn up," Beaver said, trying to comfort Queenie. "You know your little brother. Remember how he turned up in the Limehouse laundry, when we thought we'd lost him?"

"That's right," said Rosie, trying to sound cheerful. "He saved my bacon then, and no mistake."

"Sure and I'll never forget the way he climbed up that crane," added Gertie. "I couldn't have done it better myself. He's a brave lad, so he is."

"Yeah. Too brave sometimes," Queenie replied. "Too brave for his own good. Always has been."

"Come on," said Beaver. "Let's get back to HQ. Wiggins'll know what to do. And you never know – Shiner might be there waiting for us."

But of course Shiner was not waiting for them at HQ, and nor was Wiggins, who at that very moment was creeping into the Dungeon of Horrors to get the diary from Alwyn Murray's desk.

Even though Wiggins was getting quite used to the Dungeon, it still felt spooky. Thinking he could hear a rustling sound behind him, he looked back over his shoulder, and in doing so he bumped into the highwayman's skeleton, setting it swinging eerily in its gibbet. He hurriedly brushed past it, trying not to look at the grinning skull with its empty eye sockets under the black three-cornered hat. Grabbing the book from the desk, he retreated as fast as he could.

*   *   *

Shiner woke up with a start to the sound of footsteps on the stairs. Bored with sitting alone with nothing to do, he had lain down on the bed and fallen asleep, but now he quickly came to his senses and sat up. The room was dark, but he could see a sliver of light under the door and hear a key being turned in the lock. He thought fast – if he was quick enough when the door opened, he might be able to dive past Blackbeard and make his escape down the stairs. He hopped off the bed to be ready, but when the door did open there were two people standing there, Blackbeard and the chestnut-haired woman. Between them they completely blocked his way, and Shiner knew he stood no chance of getting past. The woman raised the paraffin lamp she was holding, to see better, and stared at Shiner.

"It is a child!" she exclaimed in a strong foreign accent. "A street urchin. What you do, Ivan, locking up innocent children?"

"He is no innocent," Blackbeard spat. "He was following me."

"Hah! He probably wanted to pick your pocket."

"'Ere!" Shiner protested. "I ain't no dip!"

"Dip?" the man asked, puzzled.

"Cor blimey, don't you know nothin'? A dip's a pickpocket. And I ain't no thief, so you better watch what you're sayin'."

"Hmm," the woman mused. "He is sharp, this one. You are right, Ivan – perhaps he is not so innocent."

She looked steadily at Shiner. "If you are not dip, what are you?"

Shiner looked steadily back at her, determined to give nothing away. "I'm a shoeshine boy. I clean shoes."

"Why you follow my friend? You want shine his shoes?"

"Well," said Shiner, looking down at the man's scruffy boots, "they could do with a good rub up…"

"Where your brushes? Your boot polish? No, you don't want clean his shoes. So why you follow him? Someone send you to spy on him. On *us*. Who? Tell me."

Shiner shook his head stubbornly. "No," he said. "Can't."

"Can't? Or won't."

Shiner shrugged but still stayed silent.

"Very well," the woman snapped. "You stay here till you tell. Come, Ivan!"

And with that, she left the room. Blackbeard followed, slamming the door and locking it.

Shiner was left alone again, and the attic room seemed darker than ever.

Glad to be out of the Dungeon, Wiggins hurried back to Mrs Pettigrew's shop and handed the diary to Murray, who opened the book and began to read.

"Is it real?" Wiggins asked.

"Yes," said Murray, visibly upset. "This is my poor brother's handwriting. I can hardly bear to look at it."

He blinked back a tear. Wiggins felt uncomfortable, watching his distress.

"Listen," he said. "It's getting late. I'm going back to HQ, to see what the rest of the Boys've bin up to."

"Good idea. I'll need a little time on my own to read this carefully."

Wiggins opened the door and squinted out to make sure the coast was clear. "Right," he said. "I'll be here first thing in the morning to put it back afore Madame comes to open up." And he slipped quietly out into the night.

When the Boys started getting up the next morning and Shiner had still not come home, Queenie was worried sick.

"I'm goin' back to that caff," she announced. "To see if anybody knows where he might be."

"Be careful," Beaver warned. "It might be dangerous."

"I don't care. I gotta find him."

"I'll come with you," said Wiggins. "But I gotta go back to the Bazaar first."

"We'll all go to the caff now," said Gertie. "We'll see you there."

When Wiggins arrived back at Mrs Pettigrew's shop, Murray was not looking happy. "I think I know where he was seen," he told Wiggins.

"Where?"

"The fair on Hampstead Heath." Murray opened the book at a page he had marked and began to read aloud: *"A splendid day spent enjoying all the fun of the fair. Little Sarah squealed with delight at the merry-go-round. Evie was intrigued by the Ghost Show and especially our very first glimpse of the latest invention, moving pictures."*

"Moving pictures?" Wiggins said. "Cor, I'd like to see that. But anyway, now we know where they was..."

"I'm afraid it doesn't really help us."

"Why not?"

"They went there on Bank Holiday Monday – along with half the population of London."

"Oh, yeah," Wiggins said. "I see what you mean."

"Thousands and thousands of people from all over the city."

"And it could have been any one of 'em."

"Yes. Ah, well, the diary was a good idea. Not your fault it was no use in the end."

"I'm sorry about that. Now let me put it back afore anybody notices it's missing."

Murray handed the book to Wiggins, who headed for Madame Dupont's waxworks once again. Now that it was getting light, the Dungeon didn't seem quite so spooky. He replaced the diary on the desk and turned to leave. As he did so, he noticed that the highwayman's hat had fallen off. He must have knocked it last night when he bumped into it in the dark. He bent down to pick it up, pausing to straighten the sign beside the exhibit – and stopped, staring at its words:

The body of Black Jack Duvall, hanged at Tyburn in 1740 for highway robbery, was displayed in this gibbet on Hampstead Heath, where he operated from the notorious tavern known as The Spaniards Inn.

"Blimey!" Wiggins gasped, hardly able to believe what he had read. "Spaniards!"

BLACKBEARD'S

"I got it!" Wiggins burst excitedly into Mrs Pettigrew's shop. "I found the answer!"

Murray sat up, startled. "What the…?" he exclaimed. "What are you talking about?"

"I know what 'Spaniards' means!"

"You do?"

"It's a pub. Or it was in 1740."

"It still is. It's quite famous. Of course!"

"D'you know where it is?"

"Yes. It's—"

"On Hampstead Heath, right? Where your brother went to the fair."

"My goodness! But how…?"

Wiggins quickly told him about the sign next to the highwayman in the Dungeon.

"That's amazing," Murray said. "But we still

don't know if the two things are connected."

"They must be," Wiggins replied. "All we gotta do is find out how."

Murray smiled at his confidence. "Oh, is that all? And what about the other part of the message?"

"Yeah, well … maybe if we go up to Hampstead and have a sniff around…"

"You may find it crowded. It's holiday time again, and the fair will be on. Besides which, you don't even know what you're looking for."

"That's true," Wiggins admitted. "This calls for a bit more thinking about."

"It's a pity Mr Sherlock Holmes isn't around – from what I've heard of him, he'd be able to work it out."

"That's the trouble with Mr Holmes. He's never here when he's needed. We have to manage without him most of the time."

"Do you think you can manage without him this time?"

"Course. But I'll have to think about it a bit more. I gotta go now."

"Where to?"

"We lost one of the Boys. Looks like some of

your Russian revolutionaries might have took him."

"That's terrible! Some of these reds can be quite ruthless. I couldn't bear it if anything dreadful were to happen to one of you on my account. We must find him before it's too late."

Queenie and the others were waiting outside the Russian tea room when the stern-faced waitress arrived to open up for the day. She looked at them with suspicion.

"More of you, huh?" she asked. "What you want? Where my friend who like blini?"

"That's what we want to know," Queenie told her. "He didn't come home last night."

"He is lost?" She sounded dismayed.

"What, Shiner? He couldn't get lost round here," Gertie said. "Not in a month of Sundays."

"Knows his way around, does our Shiner," Sparrow added.

"If he didn't come home," Beaver said, "it must have been 'cos he *couldn't*. And if he couldn't, he must've been locked up or somethin'. So if he—"

"Wait," said the woman, interrupting him.

"One moment." She unlocked the door of the café and ushered them inside.

"Now," she said as she closed the door behind them, "why you think Luba know where your Shiner is?"

"Who's Luba?" asked Queenie.

"I am Luba. This my tea room."

"Oh, we thought you was just the waitress."

"Waitress, cook, bottle-washer, I am everything. Now tell me why you think I know about Shiner."

"'Cos he was followin' one of your customers," Gertie blurted out.

"Why?"

"We're not allowed to tell you," Beaver said.

"Then I cannot help you."

Queenie thought hard. She did not want to put Murray in danger – but if Shiner already was, she had to do everything she could to rescue him. She took a deep breath. "All right," she said. "We might as well come clean. We're the Baker Street Boys, and we're tryin' to help a friend of ours find out who murdered his brother."

Luba stared at her scornfully. "You think I have murderers in Russian tea room? Why?"

"'Cos when we was followin' one of the suspects yesterday, he come in here. Our friend's just escaped from Russia, and if they spot him, they'll kill him."

"Who will?"

"The Russian secret police." Beaver lowered his voice to a confidential whisper. "It's all to do with spies and secret agents and stolen plans and stuff."

"Ha!" Luba let out a hollow laugh. "You think my customers work for Okhrana?"

"What's Oker ... whatever you said?"

"Okhrana is secret police of Tsar."

"What's Tsar?"

"Not what – *who.* Tsar is Emperor of Russia. He is tyrant. We hate him. But we hate Okhrana more. They spy on us, even in London."

Gertie suddenly had an awful thought. "What if," she said, "Blackbeard thinks Shiner's spyin' on him for the Okarina thingy?"

Queenie and the others were aghast.

"Who is Blackbeard?" Luba asked.

"The geezer what Shiner was trailin'," said Gertie. "You know, him as was sittin' in the corner over there when we was in yesterday." She pointed to the table.

"Ivan!" exclaimed Luba, narrowing her eyes. "I know him. He is wild man. Come!"

She headed for the door, ushering the Boys before her.

"Where we goin'?" Queenie asked.

"Ivan's house!" she replied. Then, as they opened the door, she stopped suddenly. "Wait!" she called, then dashed across to the counter, scooped up a handful of blini from a glass case and stuffed them into her coat pocket.

"My little Shiner will have hunger," she said. "These from yesterday, but he not mind."

Wiggins arrived just as Luba was locking the door behind them. "Where you lot off to?" he demanded.

"Madam Luba knows where Shiner might be," Beaver said.

"Madam Luba?"

"I am Luba."

"Pleased to meetcha." He raised his hat as he had seen Mr Holmes and Dr Watson do when they met a lady. "I'm Wiggins, captain of the Baker Street Boys. What they been telling you?"

"Enough to know we are on same side. Come. There is no time to lose. We talk while we walk."

Luba led the Boys through Soho and into the warren of little streets beyond Shaftesbury Avenue, telling Wiggins what had happened and listening to him as he explained about the Boys' mission. At last she stopped outside a small old house with a battered front door that had once been painted red. She hammered on it with her fist, and shouted, "Ivan! Ivan Ivanovich! Open up!"

After a minute or two, a man's sleepy voice from inside called, "What you want? Who is there?"

"Is Luba. I must speak with you! Open door!"

There was the sound of bolts being drawn back and then the door was opened a little way. Through the crack, the Boys could see a dark eye under a bushy eyebrow peering out at them suspiciously. Luba snorted and pushed the door wide open, to reveal Blackbeard. He looked startled to see the Boys and tried to close the door again, but Luba shoved him back and stepped inside.

"What you do, crazy man?" she demanded fiercely. "You kidnap child. Lock him up?"

"He was spying on me. Spying for Okhrana!"

"No, he wasn't!" Queenie shouted. "He was followin' you 'cos he thought *you* was spying for the Oki-whatsit."

"I do not understand."

"Never mind for now," Luba said. "Where is boy? What you do with him?"

"He is safe, locked in attic."

"Bring him," she ordered sharply. "Now!"

Blackbeard scuttled away upstairs, unnerved by Luba's ferocity. She marched into the nearest room and the Boys followed her. It was a bare room, with worn lino on the floor, a sofa against one wall and four hard chairs around a wooden table. On the table were piles of pamphlets and handbills, some in English, some in Russian, all printed in lurid red ink, echoing the colour of the flag hanging over the empty fireplace. The days and dates on a calendar hanging on another wall were also printed in bright red, in English this time, and some of the numbers had rings around them. Wiggins strolled over to look more closely at the picture on the calendar, which was of a foreign city filled with elegant white buildings and churches whose strange domes looked like golden onions gleaming in the sunlight.

"Is that Russia?" he asked Luba.

"Saint Petersburg," she answered. "Our capital city. Is beautiful, no?"

"Yes," he agreed. "I wouldn't mind going there."

"Hmm. Is pity it is home to so much cruelty, so much misery."

Before Wiggins could ask her any more, Blackbeard came back, dragging Shiner by the arm and thrusting him roughly into the room. Shiner's face lit up when he saw the Boys, but he did his best to hide his relief.

"What you lot doin' 'ere?" he asked gruffly, trying to shake off Queenie as she rushed to give him a hug.

The Boys grinned. This was the Shiner they all knew.

"Well, he's OK, at least," said Beaver. "No need to ask."

Luba stepped forward, wagging her finger at

Shiner and looking as stern as ever.

"You are very bad boy," she scolded him. "You must thank your friends for saving you. They were very worried."

"Oh, right. Thanks."

Luba shook her head in mock annoyance.

"I suppose that will have to do," she said, and pointed to the table. "Now, sit. Eat."

She pulled the blini from her coat pocket and piled them on the table in front of Shiner. This time he made no effort to hide his delight. As he tucked into the little pancakes – watched enviously by the other Boys – Luba smiled fondly at him, then turned back to Wiggins.

"You must tell Ivan everything," she said. "He will help you. He has many friends."

Wiggins hesitated. "I dunno," he said. "I promised…"

"You can trust him. The Okhrana are his most bitter enemies."

"They send secret agent here," Ivan growled. "Assassin to murder me and my friends."

"Have you told the police – *our* police?"

"They cannot help. They not believe us. We do

not know who he is, or where he is. Only that he is very cunning."

"Blimey," said Beaver, "sounds like it could be the same geezer what killed Mr Murray's brother."

"Yeah, it does."

"There has been killing?" Ivan asked. "Tell me."

So Wiggins explained everything that had happened, and Ivan listened very carefully.

"This is our man. I have no doubt it is work of Okhrana," he said when Wiggins had finished. "You have done well, but is not enough. We know there is to be meeting. We think we know where. But we do not know when."

"If only we could work out what the rest of that message means," cried Wiggins in frustration. "Three *what*, sitting *where*?"

He paced the room, deep in thought, then stopped in front of the calendar, hoping the picture of Saint Petersburg might give him some kind of inspiration. But it was not the picture that did it for him – it was the days and dates beneath it. He spun round in triumph.

"Got it!" he cried. "Look! Mon, Tues, Wed – it

ain't 'three' anything 'sat' anywhere. 'Sat' is short for *Saturday*!" He tapped the calendar with his finger. "And three can't be the date, 'cos Saturday is the ninth. It's got to be the time. So it's three o'clock on Saturday, at the Spaniards pub on Hampstead Heath!"

"Brilliant!" shouted Beaver. "Wiggins – you done it again!"

The rest of the Boys cheered. Luba smiled. Ivan nodded, then held up his hands for quiet.

"Very clever," he said. "Well done. There is only one problem."

"What's that?" asked Wiggins.

"Saturday is today. If we are to catch villains, we have no time to lose."

"Right, let's get moving, then!"

Leaving Ivan and Luba to collect up some of their friends, Wiggins and the Boys rushed back to Baker Street. As they arrived, panting, at the gates of the Bazaar, Sarge came out of his lodge, looking bewildered.

"What's goin' on?" he asked. "What's the rush?"

"We gotta get Mr Murray. We're going to the fair!"

THE GHOST SHOW

Selwyn Murray was startled when the Boys burst in on him without warning. He leapt to his feet, certain that his enemies had tracked him down and were about to murder him, so he was relieved to see Wiggins's excited face appear round the door.

"Wiggins!" he exclaimed. "What are you doing? Someone might see you!"

"Don't matter if they do," Wiggins replied. "Not now."

"What do you mean?"

"We know where they're going."

"Where?"

"The Spaniards – three o'clock this afternoon. *Saturday* at *three*. Get it?"

"Of course! Sat 3. Well done!" He pulled out

his watch. "But it doesn't leave us much time."

"You're right," agreed Wiggins. "And if we're gonna catch 'em red-handed we'll need the coppers there."

He turned to the other Boys, who were crowded behind him in the doorway, and rapped out his instructions: "Shiner, you know all about the Russians. Rosie, you know about the secret message. So you two go to Dr Watson, tell him where we're going and ask him to get on to Inspector Lestrade. Off you go, now! The rest of you, come with me and Mr Murray."

"How we gonna get to Hampstead?" asked Beaver. "It's too far to walk, ain't it?"

"It is indeed," Murray answered. "And we don't have time to wait for a train or an omnibus. We'll go by cab. Run and tell Sarge to find us a four-wheeler, quick as he can."

The driver grumbled at having to squeeze six people into his cab, but Murray pointed out that half of them were small and offered him extra money to take them all.

"And there'll be another ten shillings for you,"

he promised, "if you get us to The Spaniards Inn before three o'clock. It is a matter of national importance."

"Make it a pound and I'll have a go," the man replied.

"Very well. A pound it is. Now drive!"

Encouraged by the idea of so much money, the cabbie whipped up his horse and soon had them careering through the streets, past Lord's Cricket Ground and the elegant villas of St John's Wood, towards the long hill that led up to Hampstead Heath. It was a bumpy ride, and the Boys had to hang on tight to stop themselves being flung about inside the cab, but they all found it exciting, if a little scary.

Before they reached Hampstead, however, the poor horse began to get very tired. Its flanks were soaked with sweat, skeins of white saliva hung from its mouth and it slowed down almost to a walk. When they saw a stone horse trough by the side of the road, the driver pulled over and stopped to give it a drink of cool water while Murray and the Boys waited in an agony of impatience. Wiggins pulled out his pocket watch.

"We ain't gonna make it," he groaned.

Murray checked his own watch, then leant out of the window. "This is urgent!" he called to the driver. "Matter of life and death. We've no time to lose."

"I don't care how urgent it is," the driver replied. "It ain't worth killing my Betsy."

"He's right," said Gertie. "If she don't have a drink we shan't get there at all."

At last the driver patted the horse's quivering neck. "That'll do, girl," he said. "Not far to go now. Then you can have a rest." He climbed back onto his seat and jerked the reins. The horse responded with a steamy snort and set off again at a smart pace.

Although it was on the edge of London, Hampstead looked and felt like a village. And because this was a holiday, it was full of people who had come out of the city to enjoy the fresh air of the Heath, an area of unspoilt countryside filled with trees and ponds and green hills that were perfect for getting away from the hustle and bustle. Unfortunately, there were so many people strolling through the streets that the cab containing the Baker Street Boys and Selwyn Murray had to slow down again to get through. As it passed the ancient church, the clock was already striking three.

"Listen!" Queenie cried. "We'll be too late!"

"How much further is it?" Wiggins asked.

"At least half a mile. Maybe a mile."

"We could run that," said Beaver.

"Easy!" agreed Sparrow.

"And it'd be quicker," added Gertie.

"Right," said Murray. "Out you get!" He opened the door and called to the cabbie to stop. "Here," he said, giving him a handful of money. "Good man. You did your best. Thank you."

The Boys tumbled out of the cab.

"That way," Murray shouted, pointing down a side street. "We can cut across the Heath."

It wasn't easy going – the ground was uneven and hilly – but they dashed on towards the top, making good progress. On Murray's advice, they headed towards the music and screams of pleasure which they could hear in the distance, since the fair was always held near The Spaniards. And so they pressed on. The Boys were fit and used to running, and they soon left Murray far behind as he stopped because of a stitch, holding his side in pain but waving them on.

Soon they reached the first stalls and side-shows of the fair. Just in front of them on the other side of a narrow road, beyond a small toll-keeper's cottage, they could see a white, three-storey building with a sign board on its front: THE SPANIARDS INN. They ran towards it, halting just in time before they were run down by a black coach that emerged from the inn's yard and drove off at speed.

"Look!" Sparrow shouted, pointing at the door of the carriage. It had a monogram painted on it, a curly letter "M". As the carriage passed them, the Boys caught a glimpse of the shiny, domed head and sunken eyes of the man inside. And then it was gone, rolling down the hill and out of sight.

"Did you see him?" cried Queenie. "I could swear he was laughin' at us."

"We're too late," moaned Beaver. "He's gone."

"Yeah, but what about the geezer he was meeting?" said Wiggins.

"That's right," Gertie agreed. "He might still be in the pub."

"Stay here," said Wiggins. "I'm going to have a dekko."

"But how will you know who he is?" Queenie asked.

"Dunno. Have to wait and see."

Wiggins pushed open the door of the pub and went in. It took a moment for his eyes to adjust to the dim light, made even darker by heavy black beams overhead and low ceilings stained brown by centuries of smoke from countless cigars and pipes. Through the fug of smoke he could see that the main room which he had entered was half full of men sitting at tables or in alcoves, chatting and drinking. None of the people he could see as he walked through looked suspicious, and he was about to leave when he noticed a doorway at the other end. Putting on a cool face, he ambled nonchalantly over to it and stepped through.

It was a small room with a table in the middle, on which stood a bottle of brandy and four glasses, one of them empty. Three men were sitting around the table, deep in conversation.

One was a powerful-looking man with deep-set dark eyes, long, slicked-back hair and a pointed black beard, whom Wiggins had never seen before. The other two were Sir Charles White and his manservant, Fredericks.

The man with the long hair glared at Wiggins and waved him away.

"Clear off, boy!" he snarled in a heavy foreign accent. "Get out of here!"

Sir Charles and Fredericks glanced round casually, then suddenly recognized Wiggins.

"The messenger boy!" Sir Charles exclaimed, then snapped his fingers at Fredericks. "Get him!" he barked.

Wiggins did not wait to be "got". As the three men leapt to their feet and rushed towards him, he turned and raced back the way he had come, dodging between the drinkers in the bar and diving out through the door.

"Run for it!" he shouted to the other Boys. "They're after me!"

"Who?" Beaver asked.

"Where to?" Queenie wanted to know.

"Them!" Wiggins yelled as the three men

followed him out of the pub. "To the fair! Lose yourselves in the crowd!"

"There are more of them!" shouted Sir Charles, pointing at the other Boys with his silver-topped black cane. "I want them all."

Without waiting to be told twice, the Boys ran from The Spaniards, crossed the road and headed into the fairground. The three men pursued them, with Sir Charles shouting instructions to the other two and directing them with his cane. Murray, having now got his breath back, arrived just in time to see the chase and hobbled after the men, unseen by Sir Charles or Fredericks. As it was only mid-afternoon, the fair was not really busy yet and the crowds were not thick enough for the Boys to lose themselves in.

"We gotta keep 'em running round till the inspector and his men get here," Wiggins panted.

"And Blackbeard Ivan and his lot," Queenie added. "They'll know what to do."

"Just don't get caught, any of you," said Wiggins. "Now, scatter!"

All seven Baker Street Boys ran in different directions. The three men split up and tried to follow. The chase wound in and out of hoop-la and roll-a-penny, hook-a-duck and skittles, and dozens more sideshows and stalls. They ran around the tall helter-skelter, where girls screamed and clutched their skirts to stop them flying up as they corkscrewed down the slide; they hopped on and off the gallopers and round-abouts and swing-boats; they ducked behind the huge wheels of traction engines that puffed out steam and smoke as they powered the rides and the lights and the organs blasting out merry music. They passed the little German band that they had seen near the Bazaar, marching and playing hopefully, trying to make itself heard above the general din. It was fighting a losing battle but was still managing to collect a few pennies from young men eager to impress their girls with a show of generosity.

The Boys were starting to enjoy the excite-ment of what was turning into a great game of tag – but it was a dangerous game, with serious penalties. When the dark-eyed man finally outwitted Queenie and caught her, Beaver heard her scream and ran to her rescue. But although he was easily the strongest of the Boys, he was no match for the powerful foreigner. Without letting go of Queenie, the man shook Beaver off, threw him to the ground and was just lifting his foot to kick him when he was seized from behind. It was Ivan and a bunch of his revolutionary friends, including Luba and the chestnut-haired woman.

"Orlov!" Ivan growled. "I should have known it would be you."

"You coward!" spat Luba. "Why don't you pick on somebody your own size?"

She grabbed the man's arm and Ivan delivered a hard punch to his solar plexus, then leapt on top of him and pinned him to the ground with the help of his friends.

"Is he from the Okey-cokey?" Queenie asked.

"Yes," replied Luba. "I knew him in Russia. He is Okhrana agent and spy."

"And murderer," added Beaver. "When the coppers get him he'll be hanged."

"No, no!" gasped the man as he caught his breath. "I have killed no one!"

"Yes, you have," Queenie accused. "You killed Alwyn Murray."

"I am not assassin," he protested. "Not murderer. It was not me!"

"Well, who was it, then?"

Gertie was still running nimbly through the fairground, but Fredericks had spotted her and was on her tail. As she passed the coconut shy for the second time, he stepped out from between two stalls and grabbed her by the arm. She struggled and tried to wriggle free, but it was no use.

"Leave her be!" a loud Irish voice suddenly roared. "Take your filthy hands off moi girl!" The shout came from a big man with a mop of ginger curls who was running the coconut shy. Fredericks took no notice and tried to drag Gertie away, but the red-haired man snatched a wooden ball from his stall and hurled it with all his might. It flew like a rocket, with deadly accuracy, and hit Fredericks on the back of his head, knocking him out cold. He fell to the ground as though he had been poleaxed.

"Every ball a coconut!" the Irishman bellowed triumphantly, running forward with his arms outstretched.

Gertie spun round and let out a great shriek. "Da!" she screamed. "Oh, Dada, is it really you?"

"It is, it is!" he cried, enveloping her in a great hug. "Oh Gertie, my little Gertie! I been searchin' high and low for you since they let me out of jail. I thought I'd lost you for ever!"

And they hugged and kissed and held each other tight as though they would never let go, weeping tears of joy at being reunited.

Unlike his two companions, who had rushed around the fair like maniacs, Sir Charles was hunting his prey by stealth. He was determined to catch Wiggins himself, and planned to take him by surprise. Keeping out of sight, he crept between the stalls and tents until eventually he spotted the leader of the Baker Street Boys by the massive, ornate facade of what looked like a full-size mobile theatre. Wide steps led up to the ticket booth and entrance, where a placard announced: *Next performance 15 minutes.* The gaudy sign over the front, surrounded by pictures of ghouls and spectres of all sorts, proclaimed it to be the Ghost Show.

As Wiggins stopped before it, Sir Charles leapt

out of hiding and confronted him. Before Wiggins could run, Sir Charles took hold of his cane, pulling it apart to reveal a gleaming steel blade, which he now pointed at him.

"Blimey," said Wiggins. "A sword-stick!"

"Yes," hissed Sir Charles. "And it is razor-sharp. So stand still and do exactly what I tell you."

"Not on your nelly!" Wiggins replied. And he spun round and bounded up the steps through the curtained doorway.

Sir Charles let out a curse and rushed after him. As the theatre was between shows, the stage was empty and there was no audience in the auditorium. But it was filled with long benches and Wiggins was able to dodge Sir Charles by clambering over and around them more nimbly than the older man. Then one of the benches tipped over and Wiggins stumbled and fell. Before he could get to his feet again, Sir Charles was standing over him, the sword pointing at his chest.

"Now," he demanded. "Tell me – who sent you?"

"I did!" boomed a new voice, echoing hollowly through the theatre.

Sir Charles looked up to see Murray standing on the stage, glaring down at him with a face like thunder. All the blood drained from Sir Charles's own face as he stared in terror.

"No!" he gasped. "It can't be! It's not possible – you're…"

"Dead?" Murray taunted him.

"Yes. I *know* you are. I… I…"

"Killed me?"

Sir Charles was trembling with fear as he answered. "Yes."

"Say it again. Louder."

"I killed you. You can't be here… This is some sort of ghost show trick. Well this time I'll make sure!"

And with that, Sir Charles dropped his sword, reached into his pocket and pulled out a revolver. Raising it in front of him he took careful aim at Murray and squeezed the trigger.

There were two loud bangs at almost the same moment. The first was the gun going off; the second was the shattering of a very large mirror. Suddenly the stage was empty apart from the shards of broken glass. There was no sign of

Murray. Sir Charles spun round in disbelief as another new voice spoke up behind him.

"Yes, Sir Charles. It *was* a ghost show trick. All done with mirrors. Now if you don't mind, I'll take the gun." It was the leader of the little German band speaking. But the voice was that of Sherlock Holmes. He reached out and took the revolver, then handed it to Inspector Lestrade, who was standing beside him.

"Sir Charles White," pronounced Lestrade, "I arrest you for the murder of Mr Alwyn Murray and his wife and child."

Sir Charles glared furiously at him, quite unrepentant. "It was a mistake," he snarled, "a ghastly mistake. How was I to know—"

"That I had a twin brother?" asked Murray, emerging from where he had been standing in the wings, with Sparrow by his side.

"You!" hissed the murderer.

"Yes. You thought I was rotting in a Siberian prison camp after you betrayed me to the Russians. But I escaped, to see you brought to justice – with the help of my young friends from Baker Street."

EUREKA!

After Orlov and Fredericks had been arrested –
with Fredericks nursing a painful lump the size of
a pigeon's egg on the back of his head – the Boys
and their new Russian friends gathered outside
the Ghost Show. Sir Charles glowered furiously at
Wiggins as Lestrade and his men hauled him out
of the show and marched him away in handcuffs.

"How did you know we was in there?" Wiggins
asked Murray.

"Sparrow saw him chase you inside," Murray replied. "We decided to go through the side
entrance to take him by surprise."

"Well, you did that all right. But how did you
know what to do? How did you know about the
mirrors?"

"I seen it afore," said Sparrow with a big grin.

"We had a ghost show at the theatre once. Dead good, it was."

Wiggins was impressed. "You did well," he said approvingly.

"You all did well," said Mr Holmes as he removed his musician's cap and peeled off the false nose, eyebrows and heavy moustache. "I have followed your progress with great interest."

Dr Watson, who had only just arrived with Shiner and Rosie, shook his head in amazement as he watched the transformation from German bandsman to internationally renowned detective.

"Good heavens, Holmes!" he said. "I've seen many of your disguises, but this takes the biscuit. To think that I've passed you in the streets several times and never guessed…"

"I know," said Mr Holmes with a smile. "You even put sixpence in my collecting box on one occasion."

"So I did," laughed Dr Watson.

"Because we played your favourite tune," added the detective.

"Ha! And I wondered how you knew. But what were you doing?"

"I have been on a secret mission for my brother, Mycroft, who as you know holds a high government post. He suspected that someone had been stealing plans to a secret new vessel – capable of operating beneath water – and selling them for a great deal of money to the agent of a foreign power."

"Russia!" exclaimed Wiggins.

"Precisely."

"Orlov," declared Luba. "He is secret agent. Now you have him."

"But we don't have the plans," said Mr Holmes. "We need to recover them in order to safeguard the secret and prove his guilt."

Throughout this conversation Gertie's father had been standing to one side with his arm around his daughter, holding her tight as though afraid she might disappear again. He cleared his throat and spoke up.

"Would you be talkin' about that Russki feller with the little pointy beard?" he asked.

"That's him," replied Mr Holmes. "It would appear that he has been living among your people, using the fairground as his cover."

"He has, he has! I always thought there was somethin' fishy about him, but I couldn't fathom what it was."

"P'raps he's got the plans hid in his caravan," said Beaver. "You could show us which van is his and we could search it."

"You could," said Gertie's father, "but I doubt you'd find anythin' there."

"Exac'ly," agreed Wiggins. "First place anybody'd look."

"Right. But I reckon I know where they might be. A couple of days back I was out on the Heath in the middle o' the night, lookin' to catch a rabbit or two for the pot..."

"Not poachin' again, Da?" Gertie teased.

"This is no private estate," he said defensively. "It's public land and there's thousands o' rabbits runnin' wild out there for the takin'. Anyways, I was settin' my traps when I hear somebody comin', tippy-toeing like a leprechaun in the dark—"

"Orlov!"

"Who's tellin' this story? You or me?" said Gertie's da gruffly, but his eyes were twinkling as he spoke. "Aye, you're right, it was your man.

He didn't see me, I made sure of that, but I seen him. He was carryin' a spade and a smallish box. I saw him mark out a spot, then dig a hole and bury the box."

"You didn't look to see what was in it after he'd gone?" asked Wiggins.

"None o' my business. And whatever it was, I didn't want to get mixed up in it. I never liked the look o' that feller."

"Well, like it or not, my friend, you're mixed up in it now," Mr Holmes said. "Do you think you could find the place again?"

"Sure and don't I always need to know where my traps are? I've got one set not three feet away from that very spot."

Gertie's father fetched a spade from his own van and led them out of the fairground and across the Heath. To the Boys it seemed like a wilderness, but the Irishman knew exactly where he was going. Using various trees as markers, he eventually arrived at a secluded spot, where he pulled back the lower branches of a bush to reveal a newly turned patch of ground. Once he started to dig, it was only a few seconds before the clink of metal on metal could be heard. After a few seconds more he had pulled a black tin box out of the ground and was brushing the dirt from its lid.

"It's locked," he announced. "Shall I smash it open?"

He went to raise his spade, but Mr Holmes stopped him.

"No need for violence," he said. "If you will permit me, madam?" He stepped across to Luba, pulled a hairpin from her head and handed it to Wiggins. "Now, my young friend, let's see if you can remember what I taught you about locks."

Wiggins took the hairpin, inspected it, then carefully bent it out of shape. Concentrating hard, his tongue peeping out from between his lips, he slid the end of the pin into the lock on the box and began to move it around, up and down and from side to side, wiggling and twisting it gently. At last there was a satisfying *click* and a smile spread across his face as he lifted the lid. Mr Holmes nodded his approval and bent over the open box to examine its contents.

"Eureka!" he said, smiling.

The Boys stared at him.

"I reek of what?" Wiggins asked, sniffing.

"No, no. You don't smell of anything. What I said was 'eureka'. It's ancient Greek, meaning 'I have found it'."

Wiggins laughed. "Eureka. Yes, we have eureka-ed it, ain't we!"

"Unless I am very much mistaken, these are the missing plans. Which means that Sir Charles White must be the traitor who stole them and sold them to the Russians, through Orlov." Mr Holmes turned to Murray and held out his hand. "I congratulate you, Mr Murray. Your suspicions were correct and I am deeply sorry that you suffered such a grievous loss because of them."

"Thank you, sir. You are very kind."

"Wait a minute," said Beaver, looking worried. "What about the other bloke – Mr Redman?"

"Completely innocent," said Mr Holmes. "All he has done is support a group of Russian exiles – our friends here – who seek justice and freedom from tyranny for their homeland."

"But how does Moriarty come into it all?" asked Queenie.

"In his usual way, I have no doubt. He finds someone who desperately needs money or is greedy for more than they have, or someone who has a guilty secret that would ruin them if it were to come out. He then turns them into his puppet, doing whatever he wants while he pulls their strings. But he always operates out of sight, in the shadows, where no one can touch him."

"One of these days we'll get him," said Wiggins.

"One of these days, maybe. But now it's time to go home. You have done well once again, and you deserve your usual reward. Where shall we hold our feast this time?"

"There's only one place we *could* have it," piped up Shiner.

"That's right," agreed Queenie. "Luba's Russian Tea Room!"

Luba's usually stern face broke into a wide, beaming smile. "Yes!" she promised. "I make you real Russian banquet. You eat so much you will not be able to move!"

As an extra reward before they returned home, Murray took the Boys back to the fair and paid for them to go on all the rides and into all the sideshows. In fact, because Gertie's dad worked on the fair, most of the showmen let them ride for free, which made it all the more special. The one thing they couldn't see, of course, was the Ghost Show, which was now out of action. They found the owner busy clearing up the broken mirror, but when Murray and Wiggins went to apologize, he seemed remarkably cheerful.

"Don't worry," he told them. "I've been plannin' to make some changes anyway. The old ghost shows have had their day. I'm goin' to show something new, the latest invention – movin' pictures. They'll be the wonder o' the modern age. Folk will flock to see 'em, just you wait and see. Moving pictures! They're the future!"

Murray wished him luck, then turned to Wiggins. "Time we were heading back," he said. "We still have something to do – something very important."

Madame Dupont was in the Dungeon of Horrors, carefully cleaning the models at the end of the day with a feather duster. She was just tidying the hair on the waxwork of Alwyn Murray, when she heard a sound behind her. She turned – and found herself looking into the identical face of Selwyn Murray. She let out a scream, dropped her duster and fainted.

"Would you like a glass of brandy?" Wiggins asked her when she had come round.

"Ooh, yes, please," she said, still shaking. "I need one!"

"Just like Sarge did," Wiggins reminded her.

"I am very sorry," said Murray apologetically. "I really didn't mean to give you such a shock."

"But you… You're real? Not a ghost?"

"No, a twin. Real flesh and blood."

"It was this Mr Murray what Sarge saw the other night," Wiggins told her. "So he didn't see a ghost and he wasn't drunk."

"At least, not until afterwards," added Murray. "I'm afraid it was all my fault."

Wiggins brought Madame Dupont a glass of medicinal brandy, and between them he and Murray explained everything. Murray assured her that Sarge had played an important part in the unmasking of the real murderer of his brother and the capture of a Russian spy, and Wiggins persuaded her to relent and let him keep his job. When they told him the news, Sarge was delighted – but decided that this time it was probably better not to celebrate with a drink.

Later that evening, the Boys celebrated with the banquet that Luba had promised them in the Russian Tea Room. She had pushed the little tables together to make one long table down the middle of the room, and it was heaped with dozens of dishes piled high with different foods in the best Russian tradition. All the food was delicious, and the Boys ate and ate until even Shiner could eat no more.

After they had finished their meal, there was a moment of sadness when Gertie left, though all the Boys were happy to see her reunited with her father. Queenie and Rosie both sobbed their hearts out, and even Wiggins and Beaver found themselves blinking back tears. The six of them stood in the doorway to the café and waved goodbye as Gertie walked off down the street, having promised to come back and see them whenever the fair was in London. Each of the other Boys secretly wished that it was him or her going home with a father or mother, but it made them all the more glad to have each other.

Queenie noticed Luba looking wistfully at Shiner.

"Why are you so fond of my brother?" she asked.

"When I was young," Luba said, "I also had little brother. He look just like Shiner."

"Where's your brother now?"

"He took sick and die, many years ago, in Okhrana prison camp. But every time I look at Shiner, I see him." She squeezed the boy's shoulder. "You come see Luba again. Any time, yes? I give you lots blini, and tea with plenty sugar lumps. OK?"

Back in HQ, the Boys crashed wearily into their beds and were soon all fast asleep. All, that is, except for Queenie and Beaver. Although she was tired out after the events of the day, Queenie could not help staring at Gertie's empty bed with a mixture of sorrow and happiness. She was also watching Beaver as he took an exercise book and sat down at the table, sucking his pencil, ready to start writing. Tiptoeing across to him, she looked over his shoulder at the empty page.

"Can't think what to call this one?" she whispered.

"It's hard to choose," he replied. "There's so much that's happened, what with spies and traitors and secret messages and murders and twins and everythin'."

"Well, it all started with a ghost in Madame Dupont's Dungeon, didn't it? So how about 'The Haunted Horrors'?"

Beaver thought for a moment, then nodded. "Yeah. 'The Case of the Haunted Horrors.' That'll do nicely."

And he bent over his exercise book and began to write.

THE SPANIARDS INN AND
HAMPSTEAD

THE SPANIARDS INN is a real pub on the northern
edge of Hampstead Heath. No one is sure how it
got its name, but at nearly three hundred years
old it is one of London's oldest inns. During the
eighteenth and early nineteenth centuries it was
well known as the haunt of highwaymen and cut-
throats preying on travellers heading into or out
of London across the Heath: the notorious Dick
Turpin is said to have been one of them. The
inn is supposed to have had a number of secret
tunnels leading from its cellars onto the Heath,
to allow highwaymen to escape unseen in the
event of a raid by the law.

Hampstead still has the feeling of a village,
even though it is now simply part of north-west

London. The Heath remains a largely natural and unspoilt open area where city dwellers can enjoy walking, swimming in one of its natural ponds, and various other leisure activities. A travelling fair has traditionally been held there for centuries and still takes place on most public holidays, attracting large crowds.

ANTHONY READ studied at the Central School of Speech and Drama in London, and was an actor-manager at the age of eighteen. He worked in advertising, journalism and publishing and as a BAFTA-winning television producer before becoming a full-time writer. Anthony has more than two hundred screen credits to his name, for programmes that include *Sherlock Holmes*, *The Professionals* and *Doctor Who*. He has also written non-fiction, and won the Wingate Literary Prize for *Kristallnacht*.

The seven Baker Street Boys books are based on Anthony's original television series for children, broadcast by the BBC in the 1980s, for which he won the Writers' Guild TV Award. The series was inspired by references to the "Baker Street Irregulars", a group of young crime-solvers who helped the detective Sherlock Holmes in the classic stories by Sir Arthur Conan Doyle.